Red
Dragon Codex

RED DRAGON CODEX

BRONZE DRAGON CODEX
July 2008

BLACK DRAGON CODEX
October 2008

RED
DRAGON CODEX

R.D. Henham

MIRRORSTONE

Red Dragon Codex

©2008 Wizards of the Coast, Inc.

All characters in this book are fictitious. Any resemblance to actual persons, living or dead, is purely coincidental.

This book is protected under the copyright laws of the United States of America. Any reproduction or unauthorized use of the material or artwork contained herein is prohibited without the express written permission of Wizards of the Coast, Inc.

Published by Wizards of the Coast, Inc. MIRRORSTONE and its logo are trademarks of Wizards of the Coast, Inc., in the U.S.A. and other countries.

All characters, character names, and the distinctive likenesses thereof are property of Wizards of the Coast, Inc.

Printed in the U.S.A.

Text by R.D. Henham with assistance from Rebecca Shelley
Cover art by Vinod Rams
Interior art by Todd Lockwood
Cartography by Dennis Kauth
First Printing: January 2008

9 8 7 6 5 4 3

––

Cataloging-in-Publication Data is available from the Library of Congress

––

ISBN: 978-0-7869-4925-0
620-21622720-001-EN

U.S., CANADA,   EUROPEAN HEADQUARTERS
ASIA, PACIFIC, & LATIN AMERICA   Hasbro UK Ltd
Wizards of the Coast, Inc.   Caswell Way
P.O. Box 707   Newport, Gwent NP9 0YH
Renton, WA 98057-0707   GREAT BRITAIN
+1-800-324-6496   Save this address for your records.

Visit our web site at www.mirrorstonebooks.com

To David Shelley,
my knight in shining armor.

—R.S.

To the "everydragon" of Krynn—
At last, your tales are being told.

—R.D.H.

Dear Honored Scribe Henham,

I was so very glad that your letter reached me! What a surprise to hear that my Practical Guide to Dragons book managed to make it all the way to the Great Library of Palanthas (last I saw it, Mother had nailed it to a wall), but I'm happy that my writings and drawings fell into the hands of a scholar like yourself.

You told me in your letter that you were interested in hearing more stories about the lives of dragons and the people who have met them. All of my adventures with dragons have been well talked about, of course, but I have an interesting story for you about an old friend of mine named Mudd. It's a thrilling tale all about a vicious red dragon, a vision of a powerful pendant, a boy who's not really a boy, and a kender who's not really a kender (though Paladine knows why anyone lucky enough to be a kender would then claim not to be one).

There's lots more to the tale, of course. I've attached all of my notes for you to read. Mudd and his companions also stopped by Palanthas, so perhaps you can ask around to learn more of the exciting details of Mudd's adventure.

That's all for this time, Scribe Henham! I'll make sure to send any more stories I stumble upon during my travels. I know you'll be dying to hear all about the other dragons of Krynn—though I hope not dying for real, since I haven't yet learned how to send letters to anyone in the Gray.

All my best,

Sindri Suncatcher

The former greatest kender wizard in all the world

(Soon to be the former former greatest kender wizard in all the world, if my journeys go as planned!)

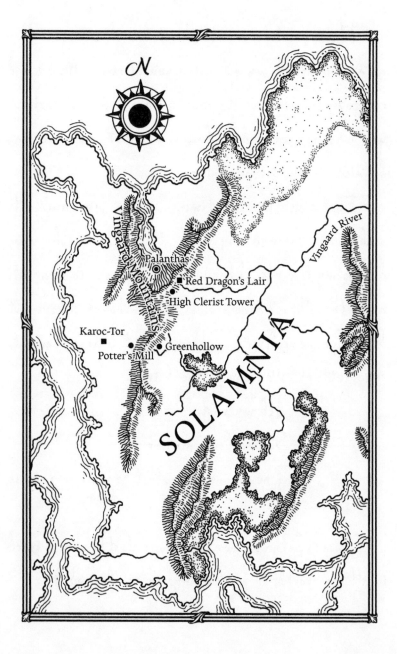

PROLOGUE

Redclaw the Destroyer licked her sharp teeth as she watched the line of men and wagons make its way along the road far below. She puffed a spurt of flame into the crisp mountain air and imagined the sweet taste of human blood on her tongue.

Digging her claws into the high rocky ledge, she uncoiled her massive body, ready to attack the unwary travelers. She enjoyed the fear her surprise attacks caused almost as much as the feast afterward.

Roaring, she rocketed from the ledge and dived for the wagons and the armed guards that accompanied them.

The humans looked up at the sound of her pounding wings and froze in terror as she released a fiery breath that ignited one of the wagons. The strong boxes in the back of a second wagon promised a welcome addition to her hoard.

She ripped the horses from their harnesses and flung them into the trees on the side of the road, saving them for later. She'd eat the humans first. Afterward, she'd carry the treasure to her lair, leaving behind nothing that would give away her existence. The last thing she needed was some nosy Solamnic Knight with a dragonlance to ruin her perfect hunting ground in the Vingaard Mountains.

Redclaw's wings whipped up a cloud of sand and pebbles from the road as she turned and attacked the nearest man. She laughed as her claws punctured his armor and sank into the tender flesh.

"Redclaw!" someone called. The sound of her name rang above the pounding of her wings and crackle of the burning wagon. She dropped the human and pivoted to face her unexpected opponent.

A gangly fifteen-year-old boy stood in the center of the road, clutching two sharp swords that looked far too heavy for his slight frame to wield. The wind from Redclaw's wings fanned his long dark hair. His silver eyes showed no fear.

"These people are mine," the boy said. "Why don't you go play somewhere else?"

Redclaw bared her deadly teeth and advanced on the pathetic human. "How do you know my name?"

The boy laughed. "You don't recognize me? Has it been so long since the war?"

Redclaw took another step toward him, testing the air for his smell, sensing the magic radiating from him.

The boy stood his ground. A loathing sneer twisted his face. "No? You don't remember me? It doesn't matter. I command you to leave."

Redclaw snorted. "You are no match for me." She sucked in a deep breath and stoked the fire in her belly.

The boy tightened his grip on his swords and set his stance. "I've been hired to protect these wagons, and I intend to do it." Magic pulsed from him, and a fine mist sprang up around them.

"Nice spell, but a little mist won't save you." Redclaw released a cone of fire into his face.

The boy dived to the side. A blast of wind turned the flames away from him. Thick clouds rolled together overhead, obscuring the sky. The scent of coming rain filled the air.

"Run!" the boy yelled to the other humans, but the dragonfear held them rooted in place. Redclaw snapped one up in her jaws.

A thunderous roar filled the air, and a sleek silver shape hurtled out of the mist, slamming Redclaw to the ground. Sharp claws scraped against her scales.

Redclaw flung her attacker off and leaped into the air, shooting a cone of fire at the annoying silver dragon that had materialized out of the clouds.

The silver dragon blocked her flames with a cone of cold air. Their two magics locked for a moment, then dissipated.

"Sleekwing Thunderbolt, how dare you come into my territory?" Redclaw roared, drawing herself higher into the air where she could maneuver better.

Below her, the humans scattered into the trees. Only the gangly boy remained on the road, his swords poised and ready to fight.

"The Vingaard Mountains are mine!" Sleekwing shouted, springing upward and clawing at Redclaw's belly.

Redclaw rolled in the air, avoiding the blow. "It's true,

then," she taunted. "I heard you'd lost something valuable in the war and had stayed behind to search for it."

"That's none of your affair." Sleekwing dived for Redclaw's neck.

"Not if I find it first," Redclaw roared. She clamped her teeth into Sleekwing's shoulder, and the two dragons rolled through the air, clawing at each other.

Redclaw felt the silver dragon's wing tear beneath her back talons. Sleekwing broke away, blood trickling from her right wing.

Redclaw bellowed in triumph, but Sleekwing filled the air with her paralyzing breath. As the cone of cold gas hit Redclaw, her muscles froze and she plunged toward the ground. Jagged pines rushed up to meet her.

Sleekwing roared and swooped down to finish her.

Redclaw regained control of her body a few feet from the ground. She arched her wings, turning the speed from her fall into forward motion. Her claws snapped around the boy's shoulders, and she swept him into the air with her.

"No!" Sleekwing roared. Her cry echoed from the mountaintops.

"It's not over!" Redclaw bellowed to her opponent. "I will destroy you, Sleekwing." Flapping hard, Redclaw sped away with the boy clutched in her talons.

Sleekwing tried to follow, but her torn wing slowed her flight. Redclaw soared to the safety of her hidden lair, already planning her revenge.

CHAPTER ONE

Mudd squirmed into the wheelhouse where the mill's crank and gears stood motionless. There was little room to maneuver in the cramped space, though he'd done it dozens of times before, unbeknownst to Master Potter, the mill's owner. Fine granules of flour dusted every surface and puffed into the air as Mudd moved, tickling his nose.

"Can you see what's broken in there, lad?" Potter asked.

Mudd ran his fingers along the familiar wooden gears. The mill wasn't as intricate an invention as something Mudd's old friend, a gnome named Hector, would have made, but it was a wonder of mechanical engineering. The mill took the force from the water flowing down the river and turned it into power to spin the giant stones that ground wheat into flour.

A sliver jabbed Mudd's finger, and he winced. "Looks like the teeth have broken off one of the gears." He worked the broken gear free and tossed it out to Potter.

"By all the Abyss," Potter swore. "It'll take me weeks to send for a new one. The village will be in an uproar."

"So will my stomach, without Hiera's bread." Mudd's sister, Hiera, cooked for him and Shemnara, the village seer.

Mudd squinted through the dust-filled shaft of light that played across the mill's guts. In his mind he traced the way each gear moved when the mill worked. He'd played this game before. What if that gear were here instead of there? If he changed the angle of turn that way, would the mill work more efficiently? Fearing the wrath of Mayor Shelton and everyone else in town, he'd wisely left his imagined fixes only in his mind—until now.

Stifling a laugh, he repositioned one of the gears. "Start it up, Master Potter. I think I've fixed it."

"What do you mean you fixed it? I got a broken gear in my hand and a full load of wheat that isn't going to get milled."

"Just try it." Mudd coughed and rubbed at the fine dust that had settled over his face.

Muttering, Potter released the brake on the water wheel. The lumbering wheel creaked and groaned as the river pushed it up and around.

The damp scent of water wafted to Mudd, and then the gears started turning, one after another. The heavy stones that ground the flour thundered into action.

Mudd shouted in triumph and worked his way out of the wheelhouse.

Potter stood scratching his head, staring from the broken gear in his hand to the twisting millstones and back. A frown creased his face. "Them millstones are going the wrong direction."

"Is there some law that says a millstone can only grind wheat clockwise?" Mudd asked.

"Well no," Potter stammered. "It's just . . . I never—"

Mudd slapped Potter on the back. "If it bothers you too much, I'll fix it back as soon as you get a replacement for the broken gear."

"Fine," Potter grumbled. "I guess you really can fix anything. And all this time I thought you only had your mind bent on mischief."

Mudd choked back a laugh. If only Potter knew all the mischief he'd dreamed of in connection with the mill.

"I better get going," Mudd said, rubbing his hands together. "I promised Shemnara I'd fix the loose tiles on her roof today."

He took a step toward the door, and his heart flip-flopped. Fear descended on him, freezing him in place. A blast of wind rattled the mill, and a sulfury smell filled the air.

Through the window, Mudd saw a huge red dragon plunge from the sky over the river, taking a deep breath as she flew toward the mill.

"Run!" Mudd yelled. He forced his feet to move, barreling into Potter and sending them both sprawling out the door just as the dragon torched the mill with a great fiery breath.

Then the dragon swooped away, winging to the center of town.

Mudd ordered his body to jump up and run after her. His legs refused. Fear created by the dragon's magic paralyzed him—dragonfear.

The dragon dived into the town square, tearing apart houses, sending great spouts of flame at the inn and trading post. Screams filled the air. Within moments, most of the town of Potter's Mill had caught fire. The dragon snatched up a farmer in her jaws and devoured him.

A new fear seized Mudd. Hiera! Concern for his sister's life overcame the dragonfear. Mudd jumped to his feet and raced toward the burning town. The road stretched out in an endless length of fear and fire.

The dragon landed on top of the town hall, tearing the roof from the frame. Hoping to find some treasure inside, no doubt. Her tail whipped back and forth, leveling Mayor Shelton's burning house. With every movement, the dragon sent clouds of ash and smoke into the air.

Mudd skidded to a stop in the town square and looked up at the massive dragon. He reached for his bow, only to find he'd left it home when he went to the mill.

The dragon leaped into the air and sent a cone of flame into the row of buildings where Mudd's house stood. Mudd cried out in anguish and ran toward his burning home. Hiera raced from the house, followed by Set-ai, the old soldier and mountain man who'd raised Mudd and his sister since their parents' death. He held a loaded crossbow in his one good arm.

"Be gone, foul wyrm!" Set-ai cried as he released the bolt from the crossbow. The shaft flew toward the dragon's eye, but the dragon twisted away and the bolt pinged off the scales on its forehead.

While Set-ai held the dragon's attention, Hiera raced down the street to Mudd. Her pink dress billowed in the wind from the dragon's wings, and the ribbons in her blonde hair streamed out behind her. In her hands she carried Mudd's shortbow and her own, as well as two quivers of arrows.

"Here!" She tossed Mudd his bow and quiver and put an arrow to her string. Her arrow zipped through the air and bounced off the dragon's chest before Mudd got his own arrow out of the quiver.

The dragon roared and lunged at them. Mudd threw himself in front of Hiera to shield her from the flames.

Except none came.

The red dragon hovered in the air above them, its wings still kicking up a whirlwind that stung Mudd's eyes. It belched a guttural laugh, then lifted into the sky and flew to the edge of town.

Black smoke filled the street. Flames leaped to the sky. Hot ash floated on the air, burning Mudd's face. He choked and reached for Hiera.

She wrapped her arms around him in a tight hug, her bow pressing into the small of his back. "Oh, Mudd, that was such a brave and stupid thing to do."

Mudd struggled out of her grasp. "Hiera, if you hadn't shot the dragon, it wouldn't have come after you. Talk about stupid."

"It was about to eat Set-ai," Hiera squeaked. Her high-pitched voice grated on Mudd's frazzled nerves.

Set-ai lumbered down the street to them. "You two all right?" The smoke made his voice sound gruffer than usual. Ash smudged his green armor.

Mudd nodded. He looked toward the edge of town, past townsfolk running to draw water. The dragon's red wings curved in a steep dive over Shemnara's house. A spurt of flame lit the sky.

"Shemnara!" Mudd cried, racing after the dragon. Shemnara relied on Mudd as if he were her own son. Mudd had no idea if the old woman would be able to get out in time.

Hiera and Set-ai followed. A burning building collapsed as Mudd passed, shooting sparks into the air and sending a flaming beam crashing into the road in front of him. Mudd leaped over it and kept going.

He rounded the corner and raced along Shemnara's street. Hungry flames devoured the house across the street.

"Look!" Hiera cried. Shemnara's door lay in splinters on the front porch.

Mudd ran up the steps and into the house. Upon first glance, his heart sank.

The soft chairs that usually sat in a ring around the hearth were splintered and overturned. Great gouges had been dug in them. The bearskin rug had been flung aside, and drops of blood stained the floor. Behind Mudd, Set-ai swore, loading his crossbow.

"Shemnara!" Mudd cried. He flew through the kitchen to Shemnara's shrine on the far side of the house.

The shrine lay empty, the stone basin Shemnara had once seen visions in overturned. Drops of blood covered the floor. The coppery scent of it twisted Mudd's stomach.

Shemnara was gone.

A scrap of parchment lay on the floor beside the basin, bearing a message in Shemnara's hand. The ink was still wet.

> *Mudd,*
>
> *Help me, or I'll be killed.*
>
> *Seek the silver dragon.*

CHAPTER TWO

Mudd sucked a sharp breath through his teeth. Shemnara was gone, and he had to save her.

Set-ai pried the note from Mudd's fingers and looked it over. Growling, he gave it back to Mudd and walked back into the main room. Mudd and Hiera trailed behind, stunned. Set-ai righted a chair and ran his fingers along the deep gouges in the plush chair back.

"What is it?" Mudd asked, clutching the note. Set-ai could track just about anything. If anyone could figure out what happened to Shemnara, he could.

Set-ai frowned and pointed at the chair. "These gouges were made by heavy draconian swords."

"Draconian?" Hiera asked.

Set-ai's brow furrowed in distaste. "You're too young to remember the war against the dragonarmies, but draconians were the Dark Queen's foot soldiers. Dragon men. Nasty creatures, and a real pain to kill. If they don't turn to stone when they die, trapping your sword inside them, they explode or melt into a pool of acid. The worst ones take the form of the human who killed them, making you think your own comrade is dead. Or. . . ." Set-ai turned away, as if not wanting to dredge up anymore memories.

"Or what?" Hiera asked, her eyes round and her cheeks pale.

Mudd licked the ash from his lips. Smoke hung in the air from the fire that still crackled outside as it consumed the house across the street.

"The sivak draconians can take the shape of someone they've killed. You think you're among friends until one of them sticks a knife in your back or slits your throat while you're sleeping." Set-ai coughed and gritted his teeth.

"You think a draconian took her?" Mudd's gut wrenched.

"I didn't say that," Set-ai growled. "I can't tell for sure, but the marks here make me think it could be. And whatever it was, it was helping that dragon."

"But what could the dragon want with Shemnara?" Hiera asked. "He can't think we'd be able to pay a ransom for his horde."

"She," Set-ai corrected. "It was a female."

Mudd rolled his eyes—he didn't care whether the dragon was a he, she, or it. "Whatever the dragon wanted, Shemnara's hurt," he said. "We have to find her."

Set-ai followed the trail of blood out the front door, across the porch, and down into the street, where it ended.

Dread seized Mudd. Even he could make out the deep

gashes in the ground where the dragon had landed. Someone had forced Shemnara into the road, where the red dragon had taken her.

"I'll go after her," Mudd cried. Gripping his bow, he bolted down the street in the direction the dragon had gone.

Set-ai took two long strides and grabbed his arm, jerking him to a stop. "You'll never catch the dragon. Even if you do, you're no match for her. Let me see that note again."

Mudd handed over the parchment. His heart pounded in his ears, and he clutched the bow so hard his hand ached. Tears trickled down Hiera's cheeks. Mudd put his arm around her, but he was too tense to give much comfort.

Set-ai cleared his throat. "It says to seek the silver dragon. That makes sense. A silver dragon can defeat a red. But Shemnara seems to be referring to a *specific* dragon, not just any silver dragon. Do you know anything about this, Mudd?"

Mudd racked his memories for any time Shemnara might have mentioned a silver dragon. "Maybe." He charged back into the house and returned to Shemnara's shrine, where he wove his way past the basin and more overturned chairs to an ancient bookcase that stood in the shadows at the back wall.

Rows of leather-bound books sat collecting dust on the shelf. Though Shemnara had given up her seer sight recently for normal human eyes, she had seen visions for more than forty years before that. For each one she'd had a scribe record the vision in great detail. Shemnara had dictated the most recent books to Mudd.

He lifted one of the heavy books from the shelf. "Shemnara

had a vision a few years back. I think I remember something about a silver dragon." Parchment rustled as he opened the cover and flipped through the pages, squinting to decipher his own untidy scrawl.

Hiera inched up beside him. Pulling his arm down so she could see the book, she made a face at his less-than-perfect handwriting. "You better hope Shemnara never looks in this book now she's got her sight back."

Mudd let out a sad laugh. He'd be happy to have Shemnara scold him if he could just get her back. "Here it is," he said. He held the book up and read:

> A vision received on behalf of the boy Kirak, who came to Potter's Mill in search of the Dragon Well—a well made by ancient wizards who used dragon's blood to create a basin of cursed liquid. This well is, of course, where I received my own powers, at the terrible cost of my natural eyesight.
>
> Fearing for the boy's safety, I refused to give him knowledge of the well and sought a vision on his behalf instead.

"Oh, I remember Kirak," Hiera said, fingering her bow. "He wouldn't talk to me, and he jumped at every little noise. I felt sorry for him."

"Yes, that's him." Mudd rested the heavy book on the back of the chair. "Always had his hands on his sword hilts."

"Stop chatting and read," Set-ai said. "What does this have to do with the dragon?"

Mudd went back to the book and continued with Shemnara's account:

> *In this vision I first beheld a silver egg covered in foul green blood, sitting on an altar. Black-robed wizards surrounded it, chanting. Great evil reached inside me, twisting my soul, trying to distort me into some heinous being.*
>
> *The egg on the altar turned black and cracked open. A group of horrible monsters clawed their way out, and I realized I was witnessing the creation of the Dark Queen's loathsome draconians.*
>
> *At the moment of this hatching, the Black Robes called up abishai demons from the Abyss. The demons rose above the altar, shrieked, and dived at the hatchlings, taking over their bodies. This scene so haunted me that I wished for it to end and tried to block it from my mind, but I failed. The last of the monsters out of the egg turned on the abishai that had come for it. They fought, draconian and demon. . . . No, I can't go on describing the scene.*
>
> *When I thought I could take no more, the darkness passed, leaving only a terrible feeling of loss.*

"This is it," Mudd said, smoothing the page down flat so

he could see it better. "Next she talks about the silver dragon. Maybe this will give us some clue."

"I hope this part is not so horrid as the last bit," Hiera said. Set-ai grunted and motioned for Mudd to read on.

Mudd raised his voice, confident now that he'd found the right entry:

> Then I saw a silver dragon, sleek and beautiful, flying over the Vingaard Mountains, searching for something. Great sorrow consumed her.
>
> Using her magic she fashioned a silver pendant in her own image and bestowed upon it a piece of her soul. It could be used to call her and cause her to grant one wish for the summoner. Then she traveled deep into the earth and hid the pendant. To guard it, she set three tests—a test of courage, a test of love, and a test of truth.
>
> At the end of this vision I sensed that Kirak was meant to search for the pendant and face the tests. I could not see if he would pass them or fail, but I knew failure could mean death.

"Death?" Hiera blurted. "Mudd, you don't think Shemnara means for you to go after the pendant?"

Mudd swallowed. Shemnara had sent Kirak after the pendant, even knowing he might fail. Mudd turned the page and rubbed his fingers across the picture there.

Shemnara had drawn it during her vision. The power of the seer-sight guided her hand, though she could not see the page with normal eyes. The drawing showed a locked stone door with strange runes carved in an intricate arch above it. She'd had Mudd make a copy to give to Kirak, saying the pendant lay beyond that door.

"I have to go after the pendant, Hiera," Mudd said. "Shemnara wouldn't have left the note if she didn't think I could get it."

"Mudd's right." Set-ai sank into the overstuffed chair next to the basin. Worry and regret filled his eyes. After a long pause, he continued, rubbing the stump of the arm he'd lost. "You know I'm too old to go on a quest like this."

Mudd eased the page with the drawing out of the book, avoiding Set-ai's eyes. It was true. Set-ai wasn't up to a long, dangerous journey. He couldn't defend himself very well with one arm, a recent injury that limited the old solidier's agility. Mudd would have to do this alone. "Someone has to stay here and keep Hiera safe in case the red dragon returns," he told Set-ai.

Set-ai grunted an acknowledgment.

Hiera propped her bow against the basin, put her hands on her hips, and asked, "Do you have any idea where that stone door is?"

Mudd shook his head. "I think the runes in the picture may say, but I can't read them."

"Let me see." Set-ai held out his hand for the parchment. Mudd gave it to him and waited while Set-ai studied it.

"Stonework as fine as that has to be dwarf-made, and Shemnara said it was deep underground. Perhaps the hill dwarves at Greenhollow may know something. There are a number of caves and mines in the mountains above their village."

"Greenhollow . . . that's on the other side of the pass along the road to Palanthas, right?" Mudd asked.

Set-ai nodded.

Mudd could get there in a few days and have the answers he needed. He only hoped that it would be soon enough to save Shemnara. He could think of no reason why a red dragon would want to carry her off.

Hiera narrowed her eyes and spoke in a clipped tone. "And while you're gone, I suppose you think I should stay here and clean up this mess."

Mudd stared at the blood on the floor. "Someone has to," he mumbled. "If you have the stomach for it. I can't waste time here. Who knows what the dragon might do to Shemnara?"

"Oh, I have the stomach for that and a lot more." Hiera grabbed her bow and marched out of the shrine.

Mudd's stomach flipped and he second-guessed his decision to travel alone. He wasn't afraid, but a little friendly company would be nice. But not Hiera. He'd have to watch out for her and that would slow him down—using precious time that he needed to save Shemnara.

Set-ai watched Hiera go, then stood and clapped Mudd on the shoulder. "You've grown up a lot and have plenty of experience. If Shemnara left a note for you to find the silver dragon, then she knows you can do it. You won't let her down."

"Right." Mudd squared his shoulders and slung the bow and quiver across his back. "I'll just pack a few things and be on my way."

CHAPTER THREE

Cold wind stung Kirak's arms and face. He clutched Shemnara to his chest, holding her and himself on the dragon's back with stiff fingers wrapped tightly in the leather harness. He shuddered, remembering the dragon harness, the war, and fighting alongside Redclaw too well. He had hoped never to ride a dragon again.

Redclaw swooped into her lair, a dark cave high up in the Vingaard Mountains. Her claws clicked and sparked on the stone floor. She furled her wings and hunched down so Kirak could climb off her back and drag Shemnara with him.

Sulfury smoke rose from Redclaw's nostrils while she watched him dismount. Kirak noticed Shemnara's arm was still bleeding, and he did his best to staunch the blood.

I hate you, he wanted to scream at the dragon, but he couldn't risk her fury—she could kill Shemnara.

"Chain her securely. We don't want her to escape." Redclaw lumbered into the deep reaches of her lair.

"Does it have to be chains?" Kirak called after her.

Redclaw snorted a lick of fiery breath back at him.

Kirak stepped between Shemnara and the flames, shielding her. Redclaw's breath brushed his face, stoking his anger.

"Chains," Redclaw growled. "Good and tight. I will have my revenge, and you will have what you want as well."

Kirak led Shemnara deeper into the cave. She came without a struggle. Her only attempt to resist him had been back at the house when he ordered her to write the note for Mudd. Her disobedience had ended with an unfortunate gash in her arm from one of Kirak's swords.

She'd said nothing since then, just stared at him with her sharp eyes. Kirak had thought she was spooky when she was blind, but her gaze now made him shiver.

He took her to a small alcove just off the main cavern. Redclaw had attached several sets of chains to the wall. Skeletons from humans she'd captured in the past littered the floor.

Kirak shook his head. The cave was no place for an old woman. He pushed a pile of bones out of the way and forced her up against the wall. He found the longest chain and snapped the heavy manacle around her wrist.

She glared at him, and he thought he saw a spark of pity in her brilliant blue eyes. Pity for him? She should be worried about herself.

"Stop it," he commanded, but Shemnara kept her gaze riveted on him while he searched the room for a scrap of clean material. He found one and bandaged her wounded arm.

"Sorry about the cut. I didn't want to. I mean . . . you forced me to do it," Kirak stuttered.

"You've fallen in with some bad company, I'm afraid," Shemnara said.

Kirak stepped away from her. Bones crunched beneath his feet. "I was born in bad company."

"I know," Shemnara said, rubbing her bandaged arm.

Kirak tensed. "You know who I am, and you saw a vision for me anyway?"

Shemnara settled herself on the floor against the cave wall. "What you have been doesn't matter. You can still choose the kind of person you will be now."

"I can hardly disobey a red dragon," Kirak said. He removed the bones from the room. If Shemnara had to stay here, the least he could do was clean the place up.

Shemnara watched him work. "Are you under the dragon's magical compulsion, then?"

"No," Kirak said. He retreated deeper into the cave and searched through Redclaw's horde for bedding and other things to make Shemnara more comfortable.

"What did she promise you?" Shemnara asked when he walked back in.

Kirak gritted his teeth and arranged a bed for Shemnara without answering. He filled a pitcher with water and put it within her reach.

"There," he said. "It's the best I can do."

Shemnara laid her wrinkled hand on his arm. "Why didn't you look for the dragon pendant?"

"I did." Kirak pulled away from her. "I've spent years

looking, but I can't find it. Not on my own. If you must know, Redclaw came up with this plan to force Mudd and a dwarf named Greenthumb to help me. She's sure that together we can find it and pass the tests to claim it."

Shemnara blinked. "Kirak, why didn't you just ask Mudd to help you?"

Kirak stumbled back against the opposite wall as if she'd hit him. "Well . . . I . . . Mudd wouldn't help me. No one does anything for anyone else unless they're forced to."

Shemnara frowned. "I suppose in the dragonarmies there is no friendship or loyalty, but that's not how it is with everyone."

Kirak eased away from the cold stone. "No, I couldn't *ask* Mudd. This is the only way." He stormed out, hating Shemnara, Redclaw, and himself.

CHAPTER FOUR

The smell of smoke clung to Mudd's hair and clothes. The people of Potter's Mill had done what they could to put out the fires, but the red dragon had destroyed much of the town. A cloud of gray haze still hung in the air all the way to the mountain slopes above him.

Mudd's pack hung heavy on his back. He clutched his shortbow in his right hand, and his left hand strayed to his father's sword sheathed at his waist.

His heart pounded with each step on the road away from town. Setting out alone was harder than he thought it would be. He missed having someone to talk to and joke with. The empty road would have been fun if he had a friend walking beside him, like his gnome friend Hector.

A sliver of pain shot through his heart, and he pushed the thought away. Hector had died in a fire, and there was nothing Mudd could do to bring him back. He couldn't afford to think about that now—Shemnara was counting on him.

The road steepened and rose into tangled stands of aspen and pine trees. The rustle of new leaves fluttering in the wind made him jumpy. Golden sunlight glinted off the spring buttercups that grew in the tall grass beneath the trees.

He knew the forest above the village well. He'd climbed most of the trees and even named a few of them, like the fat old fir tree on the rise that he affectionately called the Old Man. But now, since the dragon destroyed his town, everything looked different. The forest felt exposed and dangerous.

Mudd quickened his step. The road to Greenhollow led him eastward over the Vingaard Mountains. This early in the spring, patches of snow still clung to the shady slopes above.

A twig cracked.

Mudd froze, listening.

The wind sighed through the trees. A ground squirrel raced across the road, and a chipmunk chittered from the branches above.

Perhaps the noise had been no more than a passing deer. Mudd's hand tightened on the polished wood of his bow, and he started forward. A dragon wouldn't hide in the trees.

But a draconian might. Mudd whirled around, searching the forest for any sign of the creatures Set-ai had warned him about.

Nothing. The forest seemed eerily peaceful. Mudd frowned and hurried up the road. It did no good to jump at shadows, but he couldn't shake the feeling he was being watched and followed.

He made camp just before sunset. His first instinct was to

bed down in a sheltered basin beneath the trees. He discarded it, choosing instead a slope where he could get a clear look at everything around him.

He laid out his bedroll and sat on it, pulling a hunk of salted beef and two rolls from his pack. Most of the weight in there came from food. He hated to go hungry. Cold, he could stand. No extra change of clothes, he could live with. He just couldn't face an empty belly.

After he ate, his eyes began to droop. Crickets struck up a chorus in the deepening darkness. Stars glimmered overhead. He blinked and jumped to his feet. What if something were out there? It wouldn't be safe to sleep—but how could he stay awake?

Mudd jerked awake. Morning dew clung to the spring flowers and left his clothes and bedroll damp. The hairs on the back of his neck stood on end. He grabbed his bow and put an arrow on the string. Turning, he surveyed the slope above and below.

Hummingbirds and butterflies floated from one stand of bluebells to the next. Fresh mountain air filled his lungs. The slope was empty of any foul creature that might attack him.

Mudd groaned and dropped the bow onto his blankets. "Stop making yourself crazy," he muttered.

After a quick breakfast he packed up and moved on. But

with each step he took, his feeling of being followed grew. He heard and saw no one, but he couldn't shake his paranoia.

In desperation he left the road, racing swiftly and silently beneath the trees. Like a forest animal, he hid his trail by following streams, climbing trees, and jumping across branches from one tree to the next. He figured he'd shake his pursuer in no time.

Time passed. Miles stretched out behind him. He stopped beneath a tall pine tree and stood motionless.

A foot scuffed against soft soil. Pine needles crackled.

Mudd sucked in a breath, drew an arrow, and waited.

And waited.

A drop of sap fell from the pine tree onto his arm. He flinched but held his stance. A woodpecker landed on a nearby branch and thumped away at the trunk. *Rat-a-tat-tat*. Mudd's arm shook from holding the bowstring back so long.

It didn't work. Whatever was out there could see him and knew he was waiting for it.

Mudd slipped the arrow back into his quiver and sprinted into the trees. His pursuer wasn't looking for an armed confrontation, so he'd have to plan some other form of meeting.

His mind spun with ideas while he raced ahead, trying to put some distance between himself and whoever followed. Tree branches flashed past, slapping at his legs and face. Pebbles rattled beneath his feet. He was making enough noise even a child could have found him.

The sun slid toward the far horizon. A chill pinched the air. Mudd topped a rise and started down the other side. Controlling his footsteps so they stayed silent, Mudd raced deep into the trees. Stopping in a stand of young pines, he opened his pack and set to work.

Using a light rope, he bound his sword to the top of a sapling and drew it back so the tip of the tree touched the ground. He strung the rope around the bottom of a different tree, then stretched it across the path he'd left for his pursuer to follow.

When the draconian walked into the rope, it would spring loose, causing the sapling to hurtle upright and slam the sword into the draconian's chest.

Too obvious, Mudd thought. Half a pace farther he set a second trap. He hid a rope beneath the leaves with his dagger ready to spring out and slice the draconian's neck. If it was smart enough to avoid the first trap, it was sure to fall into the second.

Still, he couldn't be too careful. Climbing a tall tree a few yards away, Mudd settled onto a branch and readied his bow. If the daggers didn't finish the creature, he'd shoot it down—he hoped.

Set-ai had insisted he should spend more time practicing with the bow, but practice was tedious, and Mudd had preferred to keep busy taking things apart to see how they worked. Despite that, he was a fair shot. From the tree, he could hardly miss.

A twig cracked near the top of the rise. A pebble rattled down the slope. Mudd drew his arrow back on the string and strained to see through the branches that obscured his view of the trail. The only place he could see clearly was where he'd set his traps.

A flock of birds fluttered up from the trees. Mudd tightened his grip on the bow. Pine needles poked his arm as the wind rustled the branches around him. Footsteps soft and quick came from the trail he'd left. He caught a glimpse of brown through the trees. Rapid, shallow breathing marked his pursuer's progress.

A few more yards. A couple of feet.

A small figure pushed through the saplings, running fast and quiet. Its brown and green clothes blended into the forest.

At the instant the figure stepped across the first rope, Mudd got a clear view.

"Hiera!" he screamed.

Chapter Five

The first sapling snapped up, plunging Mudd's sword toward Hiera's heart.

Hiera twisted away and stumbled into the second trap.

The sharp blade sliced through the air, a deadly stroke that would have cut a grown man's throat. Fortunately, Hiera was a good bit shorter. The dagger whizzed over her head and stood there wobbling back and forth on top of the sapling.

Mudd dropped his bow as he jumped from the tree and raced over to his sister.

"Hiera," he said, wrapping her in a tight hug. She could have been cut down by his weapons. "Oh, my baby sister." She felt so fragile in his arms. He pressed his cheek against her soft blonde hair.

"I am not a baby." She shoved him away and picked up the shortbow she'd dropped while dodging his trap.

Mudd swallowed. He'd never seen Hiera in anything besides a dress before. She stood in front of him now wearing breeches and a green shirt covered by leather armor similar to

Mudd's. Instead of ribbons and curls, her hair was tied back in a tight bun. The bow rested in her hand as if it had been there all her life, only he'd never noticed it before. She wore a long knife sheathed on either hip. A brown cloak lay across her shoulders, and a light pack hung on her back.

"You nearly killed me," Hiera said matter-of-factly. She seemed angrier that he'd called her a baby than at his traps.

"I'm sorry," Mudd said, fingering the rope he'd tied the tree down with. "I didn't know it was you. Hiera, what are you doing here?"

"Coming with you, of course." She set to work untying Mudd's weapons from the trees.

"No." Mudd grabbed them away from her. "You're going home. You're too young for a quest like this."

"I'm as old as you were when Shemnara sent you to find someone to save Potter's Mill from the beast that killed Mama and Papa." Hiera strode over to the base of the tree Mudd had been hiding in. Picking up his fallen bow and arrow, she turned back to him. "You shouldn't leave your weapons lying around."

Mudd sheathed his sword as he spoke in a low warning voice. "Hiera, I'm going to Greenhollow alone and that's final." He snatched the bow from her hands.

Hiera glared at him, putting her hands on her hips. "Set-ai thinks you need someone with you who can wield a weapon with skill. You need someone who can follow tracks over any terrain, someone who knows the mountains and how to survive in them."

"I can do those things." Mudd puffed out his chest.

Hiera rolled her eyes. "You *might* have been able to do them if you had paid attention to Set-ai's lessons, which you didn't. You're lucky to hit a target at twenty paces, and sneaking about isn't going to feed you when your pack is empty. Since *I* paid attention, I have the skills that you lack. You need me, and I'm coming."

As Mudd stared at her, a pang of fear lanced across his chest. "Hiera, this is no game. Stop pretending to be a hero and go home. You could have died just now."

"I might have died if you were better at setting traps. As clever as this one was, it wasn't very practical. I'm coming, no matter what you say."

Mudd rolled his eyes and growled, shaking with anger. Hiera could be more exasperating than anyone. "You are not coming!"

Hiera's shrill voice answered him shout for shout. "Am too coming, and you can't stop me!"

"Oh yes I can," Mudd yelled. He grabbed at her, but she dodged away.

"If you don't let me travel with you, I'll go to Greenhollow on my own, find the pendant, and save Shemnara by myself!" Hiera's pronouncement echoed above the trees.

A low growl answered.

Mudd and Hiera froze.

Something heavy thumped against the ground in the forest ahead, followed by a second thump, then two more. A shrill hoot filled the air, then the trees shook as some large creature moved through the underbrush toward them.

"Get back." Mudd pushed Hiera behind him and readied his bow.

By the time he had an arrow on the string, a massive head stretched out of the foliage. A tangled mess of brown feathers and fur covered it, except for its red-rimmed eyes and sharp beak. It let out a harrowing squawk and lunged at Mudd.

Mudd danced back and was surprised to see that the head was not followed by a bird's body, but by that of a giant brown bear. It reared up on its hind legs, showing a regal mass of plumage and fur on its throat and torso as it growl-hooted and pawed the air with its long claws.

Mudd gasped. An owlbear.

His parents had told him stories of owlbears to scare him into being good at night. Their tales had never stopped him from sneaking out, but now that he was face to face with one, he found it far more frightening than any story.

Screeching, it came back down and charged at Mudd, its sharp front claws tearing great chunks out of the ground.

Mudd loosed his arrow. It whizzed past the owlbear's massive shoulder and clattered away into the trees. Mudd jerked a second arrow out of his quiver, but never got it to the string.

The owlbear closed the distance between them in one lumbering stride.

Gasping, Mudd dropped his bow and jerked out his sword.

The owlbear pecked at Mudd. Mudd dodged to the side, and its massive beak snapped closed in the air where Mudd had been. It hooted angrily and clawed at Mudd. Its musky scent filled the air.

Mudd swung his sword at the owlbear's claw, but the creature was faster. It caught hold of Mudd's ankle and lifted him into the air.

Mudd yelped and hacked at the claw, trying to free himself. His first blow slid off the owlbear's thick feathers. The second chop penetrated, biting into tough skin. The owlbear screeched and pecked at Mudd.

Mudd twisted away from the deadly beak as the owlbear shook him. Mudd's head snapped back and forth and he started seeing spots. The sword dropped from his limp hands.

Hooting in triumph, the owlbear opened its beak to tear out Mudd's stomach.

CHAPTER SIX

An arrow zipped through the air and buried itself in the owl-bear's eye. The owlbear squawked and dropped Mudd.

The wind knocked out of Mudd's lungs when he slammed into the ground, and he lay paralyzed for a moment.

The owlbear clawed at its eye, tearing the arrow out. Hiera's bowstring snapped again, and a second arrow plunged into the owlbear's other eye, burying itself in clear to the fletchings.

The owlbear bellowed in bitter pain and rocked back and forth.

"Run, Mudd!" Hiera yelled.

Mudd tried to get up, but his arms wouldn't move and his legs were tangled from the fall.

The owlbear thundered to all fours above him, whipping its head back and forth. Hiera's bowstring snapped twice more.

"Mudd, get out of there!" Hiera cried.

The owlbear's hoots turned to a long plaintive moan. It wavered on its feet.

Hiera reached under Mudd's shoulders and jerked him

out from beneath the owlbear. It bellowed one last time and thundered into a heap, shaking the forest floor.

"Mudd?" Hiera said. Her worried brown eyes stared down into his face.

Mudd managed to get enough air into his lungs to groan.

"Oh good, you're alive," Hiera said. She wrapped him in a tight hug. "I was afraid that monster had snapped your neck."

"I can't breathe," Mudd said, pushing her off him and gasping.

She backed away, and an awkward silence fell over them. He could tell Hiera was dying to say "*I told you so*," but was biting her tongue until she knew Mudd wasn't mortally wounded.

Mudd pressed his hand against his aching neck and sat up. His vision swam for a moment, and then cleared.

The monstrous owlbear lay in a heap of feathers and fur inches from his legs. The arrow in the eye had killed it, going straight through to the brain. Hiera's other shots had just sped it on its way.

Mudd shook his head and then regretted it as pain shot down his spine. He could never have hit such a small target as the owlbear's eye. He cleared his throat. "Hiera, I—"

"It's all right. You don't have to say it." Hiera rested a comforting hand on his shoulder.

Mudd grunted, annoyed at her superior attitude. "Yes, I do. Thank you, Hiera. You saved my life."

Hiera smiled, and her eyes twinkled. "I can't believe

you missed that shot. The owlbear was right there, as big as a cottage."

Mudd grimaced. "I said thanks. What more do you want?"

Hiera squatted down in front of him and looked straight in his eyes. "I want to come with you."

Mudd's heart raced and he clenched his fists. "This is my quest. I have to do it myself. Can't you see that?"

"Mudd." Hiera took his hand. It felt strange touching her leather gloves and bracers instead of soft skin. "I promise—"

"Promise what?" Mudd said, swallowing.

Hiera's brow furrowed. "I promise I won't die. In fact I'll do one better. I'll keep you alive as well."

Mudd glanced at the owlbear. Maybe Hiera was right.

"Let's find somewhere to camp," Hiera said. "I'll cook some owlbear meat for dinner." She pulled out one of her knives and went over to the corpse.

"I don't want to eat that thing." Mudd forced his reluctant body to stand so he could edge away. A moment before, the owlbear had tried to eat him. It didn't seem right eating it in turn.

Hiera rolled her eyes and retrieved her arrows but left the owlbear untouched. "You may wish you had later on when you run out of food."

"I've packed enough to get me to Greenhollow. You look like you haven't packed much at all." Mudd pointed to Hiera's small pack.

"I have what I need," Hiera said. "I can catch my meals as we go along."

She set out through the trees, motioning for him to follow. "When you left the road, did you have any idea where you were going?" Hiera asked.

Mudd grimaced. He'd been more interested in losing his pursuer.

"It's all right," Hiera called over her shoulder. "I know a shortcut back to the road from here. Come on."

"I'm already starting to regret this," Mudd muttered. He pushed his way through the trees to catch up with her.

The air grew chilly. It would be dark soon. The scent of pine hung heavy around him. Hiera's long knife flashed in the setting sun as she twirled it while keeping up a brisk walk.

"Where'd you get those knives?" Mudd asked.

He carried his father's sword, such as it was. Their parents had not been wealthy, but his father, like many other men from Potter's Mill, had fought in the war. His father's sword was sturdy and reliable if somewhat plain and a bit too heavy for Mudd's liking.

Hiera pulled out the other knife and spun both in her hands. "Set-ai had them made for me. Because I'm small, I need something light and easy to wield. He said he'd train me to use his dragon claws when I'm a bit bigger."

Set-ai's dragon claws looked like two heavy swords, but they curved at the top and had a sharp hook at the bottom and in the middle. The handles were attached to the back of the blades with pointed spikes for cutting downward. They were deadly weapons that Mudd had never had any desire to wield.

"I can't picture you with his dragon claws," Mudd said. He had once watched Set-ai train a girl to handle them pretty well, but that girl had been a *knight*.

Hiera grinned impishly at him and sheathed her knives. "Just wait and see." She sprinted into the trees, leaving Mudd to chase after her.

Kirak cooked a fish over the fire near the dragon lair's entrance. The juice sizzled, filling the air with a succulent aroma. His stomach grumbled for breakfast, and he told it to be quiet. The fish he'd caught was the only food available at the moment, and it wasn't going to him.

He slid it off the stick onto a shiny plate from Redclaw's horde. His stomach continued to complain as he made his way back to the main chamber and the alcove beyond where Shemnara huddled.

"Best I can do, I'm afraid." Kirak set the plate down next to the old woman.

Shemnara brushed her white hair out of her eyes and looked up. "The best thing you could do is to let me go."

Kirak backed away. The cave was damp and chilly since Redclaw wasn't there at the moment to heat it with her fiery body. "I'll try to find you another blanket," he told Shemnara.

"Kirak." Shemnara's wrinkled fingers shot out and grabbed his arm. "I know you're planning something else . . . something terrible. Don't do it. Unchain me, and we'll leave together while Redclaw is away."

Kirak shuddered and pulled out of her grasp.

Shemnara's blue eyes pierced him to the core. "People are going to get hurt, and I know you don't want that."

Kirak fled back to the main chamber and slumped against the wall.

A blast of hot air filled the cavern, and Redclaw landed in the entrance, blocking the way out. Blood dripped from her teeth. She licked it off and belched, sending a spurt of fire across the room.

"Kirak," she bellowed.

Kirak got to his feet and stepped out to face her.

"Your friend Mudd left me an owlbear to feast on. Most delicious. He's heading right where we want him, by the way." Redclaw preened in satisfaction.

"Did he see you?" Kirak asked. Icy shivers went through him, but he steeled himself for what he knew he had to do.

"No. He killed the owlbear a while ago. He's nearly to the dwarf village now. It's time to go." Redclaw hunched down so he could climb on her back.

Kirak stayed where he was. "I'm not going."

"What?" Redclaw roared and reared up over his head.

"This whole plan was a bad idea," Kirak said through gritted teeth. "I won't go along with it anymore. If you want revenge on the silver dragon, you'll have to do it by yourself." Kirak readied himself for the burst of flame that would turn him to ash.

Redclaw snorted and lowered her head to look him in the eyes. Her soft, menacing voice echoed in the silence of the cavern. "I will kill the silver dragon with or without you. But if you refuse to help me, you will never become what you were meant to be. You will spend your whole life on the ground, hated and hunted, and the very people you're trying to protect will turn on you and kill you."

Kirak blanched and stared down at his feet. He knew Redclaw was right.

"Look at me!" Redclaw's voice boomed through the cavern.

Kirak lifted his gaze and found himself staring into Redclaw's flaming red eyes. He tried to look away, but his body froze in place.

Redclaw's voice surrounded him in a hypnotic rumble. "You will do things just the way we planned. When you, Mudd, and Greenthumb find the silver dragon's pendant, you will take it and bring it to me. Kill anyone who tries to stop you."

The dragon's compulsion burned through Kirak's mind like fire.

"Now, climb on my back," Redclaw said, lowering herself to the ground.

Kirak's body moved of its own accord, pulling him up the hard dragon scales onto Redclaw while the shreds of his free spirit fled to the back of his mind.

CHAPTER SEVEN

Mudd stopped at the top of the rise with Hiera beside him. Below, the mountain sloped down into a wide hollow. A cluster of wood and stone cottages stood in the middle, surrounded by newly plowed fields.

The squat, burly dwarves were out in the fields planting their spring crops. They'd braided their long beards so they wouldn't get caught on the shovel or seed bags they carried over their shoulders. Their deep tan skin and earthy-colored clothes made them look much like the fields they planted.

Mudd grimaced. Loosening the soil with the plow was bad enough—he'd had to do it a time or two when he hadn't disappeared fast enough in the mornings—but the actual work of putting the seeds into the ground was the most tedious thing he could think of.

"Come on." Hiera set out down the hill. "Set-ai said their leader is a dwarf named Stonefist Drakecutter. If anyone around here knows where that stone door is, it's him."

Mudd fingered the folded parchment in his pocket. The

smell of dinner cooking rose up from the village. He licked his lips and strode after Hiera, catching and passing her within a few steps.

A polite inquiry with the first group of dwarves they met led them to the biggest field in the valley. A dwarf about Mudd's age—in dwarven years—and an old dwarf with gray in his beard toiled in the late afternoon sun.

As Mudd walked up, he heard the young dwarf muttering to himself. "Ha, another draconian dead at the hands of the great Drakecutter. No . . . it's still moving." The dwarf gripped the shovel's smooth wooden handle and plunged the blade into the ground, stabbing again and again in such a frenzy that his bushy brown beard threatened to come out of its intricate braids.

"A little less shovel and a little more seed, Greenthumb," the old dwarf said from the next row over. "Just think how this field will look in the fall—tall green cornstalks bending their leaves to the sun, with golden tassels shimmering in the wind. We'll harvest bushel after bushel of ripe ears."

The old dwarf dropped a seed in the ground, moved forward a step, and planted another.

"I don't care about corn." Greenthumb threw his shovel on the ground. "Farming is boring. Let me go on an adventure. I want to do something grand with my life."

Mudd stifled a laugh. Neither dwarf had noticed him and Hiera yet, and he didn't want to interrupt such an interesting exchange.

"Farming is grand," the old dwarf, whom Mudd figured

must be Stonefist Drakecutter, said. "We're planting the seeds of new life. There's nothing better." A radiant smile lit up his scarred and wrinkled face. He cradled the seeds in his rough hands.

"Maybe farming is great to you now, but you got to fight in the war. You've already proven yourself a hero. I want to do the same." Greenthumb kicked a dirt clod, spraying the brown soil into the air.

"I fought that war so you wouldn't have to," Stonefist snapped, pointing at Greenthumb. "So we could have a free land to live in and plant in peace." His face grew red, and he started planting faster. His long gray beard swayed in rhythm with his shovel and seeds.

Greenthumb threw a handful of seeds in the hole and kicked dirt over the top. "After the fields are planted. Just let me go for a few months. As long as I take Drakecutter, I'll be safe."

"No!" his father said. He dropped the shovel and bag of seeds and marched over to Greenthumb. "You will never, ever touch my axe."

He shook his stout fist in Greenthumb's face and growled. "It is magic, blessed by Reorx, the god of crafting, but I paid a high price for that blessing. My own blood quenched it in the forging. The magic gives it power to cut through dragon scales, but if the axe is ever lost or broken, the Drakecutter family will be doomed."

Silence fell over the field.

Mudd cleared his throat. "Master Drakecutter, may I have a moment?"

Greenthumb whirled around, startled. His face went red

when he saw Mudd and Hiera. He picked up his shovel and went back to planting, grumbling under his breath.

"Yes, children? What can I do for you?" Stonefist answered, stepping over the furrows to Mudd and Hiera.

Mudd bit his tongue to keep from objecting at being called a child. But Stonefist *was* likely to be well over three hundred years old. Compared to that Mudd and Hiera were children indeed.

Mudd reached for the parchment in his pocket. "I was wondering if you'd ever seen—"

A shadow passed over the sun, and Stonefist looked up. "By all the Abyss," he growled.

A bolt of fear went through Mudd. He knew what he would see before he wrenched his gaze to the sky. A rush of hot air hit Mudd as the same red dragon that had destroyed Potter's Mill passed overhead, roaring toward the dwarf village. Mudd stood paralyzed for a moment.

Greenthumb fell to his knees. Hiera pulled an arrow from her quiver with shaking hands, put it to the bowstring, and headed after the dragon. A cone of fire shot from the dragon's wicked jaws and seared a row of houses.

Stonefist shook himself and sprinted for town. "Not my village," he shouted. "Get away, you foul beast!" He passed Hiera in a mad rush.

Greenthumb dragged himself to his feet and started after his father at the same moment that Mudd mastered his own fear and raced after Hiera.

The red dragon snapped up a dwarf that ran from a burning

house. The dwarf's scream ended as it disappeared down the dragon's throat. She roared in delight and breathed out another jet of fire. Stone cottages melted in the heat from her breath. The stench of sulfur and burning rock filled the air.

Step by step, Mudd forced himself toward the red monster. His heartbeat thundered in his ears, drowning out the screams of the dwarf villagers.

Stonefist ran toward the largest house at the edge of the village. Hiera dropped to her knees behind a dirt embankment just outside the village and sent an arrow up at the dragon. Mudd hunched down beside her and fumbled with his own bow. Greenthumb raced into the village right behind his father.

The dragon roared and settled onto the street between Stonefist and his house. Her burning eyes stared down at the two dwarves.

Stonefist dropped his gaze to the dragon's chest, avoiding eye contact. "You've made a serious mistake coming here," he shouted.

The dragon laughed, sending a cloud of black smoke up from her nostrils. "I hear the terrible Stonefist Drakecutter has taken up farming."

"Something you should have thought of doing before coming here to meet your doom," Stonefist said.

The dragon lunged forward. A massive claw caught Stonefist in the side and sent him flying through the air. He slammed into a burning building. The structure gave way, burying him in the rubble.

"No!" Greenthumb yelled and charged the dragon, wielding the shovel he still clutched.

"And this must be little Greenthumb." The dragon lowered her head and stared Greenthumb in the eyes.

"I'll kill you," Greenthumb growled.

"With that magic axe you have in your hands?" The dragon's voice sent an eerie chill down Mudd's spine.

"Uh oh," Mudd said.

"What?" Hiera had stopped shooting since Greenthumb was between them and the dragon.

"I think the dragon just hypnotized him," Mudd whispered.

"Come on then," the dragon said to Greenthumb. "Let's see what you can do."

Greenthumb lunged forward and hit the dragon's leg with the shovel. It bounced off, vibrating so hard he almost dropped it.

"Nice try, little one," the dragon said.

Greenthumb shook his head and hefted the shovel with a puzzled look on his face.

While the dragon filled the air with hot laughter, Greenthumb darted forward. He ran up the dragon's front leg and swung the shovel with all his strength, striking at the dragon's exposed lower neck.

The weapon splintered in his hands and clattered away to the ground.

The dragon shook herself, sending Greenthumb flying. He

hit the ground on his back. Before he could move, the dragon pressed a claw over his chest, smashing the air out of him.

"You will never be half the fighter your father was," she said, sneering. "But you'll fill my needs for the time being."

Unfurling her wings, the dragon leaped into the air and soared away. Mudd jumped up and raced toward Greenthumb and the burning building that had collapsed over Stonefist.

Coughing, Greenthumb staggered to his feet and stared at the broken pieces of the shovel on the ground. A look of understanding came into his eyes. He hadn't been wielding his father's axe after all.

The red dragon had destroyed most of the village, but the Drakecutter home stood untouched. Greenthumb dashed into his house. He came back out a moment later. "It's gone!" he cried. "The axe is gone."

CHAPTER EIGHT

Mudd skidded to a stop in front of the collapsed house. Stone-fist lay unconscious in the rubble, surrounded by crackling flames. Billows of acrid black smoke filled the air, stinging Mudd's throat and making him cough. Waves of heat beat against him.

"Father!" Greenthumb screamed. He raced across the street and dived toward the fire. A couple of older dwarves caught him and pulled him away, calling for buckets and water.

No time for that.

Mudd dropped his pack and laid his bow aside. He unfastened his water skin and dumped the contents over himself, soaking his clothes and cloak. Drawing the wet cloak close to protect himself from the fire, he raced to the fallen dwarf.

Heat seared his lungs and burned his feet. As the flames surrounded him, his mind flashed back to the fire at Viranesh Keep where he'd lost Hector.

Flames raced up the third-level stairs behind him, consuming everything in their path. "Hector!" Mudd cried. He wrapped his arms around his fallen friend and dragged him out of the fire.

"What are you doing?" Hiera's shrill voice snapped him back to the present. He lowered the burned dwarf to the ground. It wasn't Hector. He couldn't go back in time and save his friend. At least he'd gotten the dwarf out.

A slap of cold water hit Mudd in the face. Only then did he realize his cloak had dried in the heat and had started to burn.

Greenthumb raced to his father's side, followed by the other dwarves.

"Help!" a plaintive cry sounded above the roaring flames.

"Mudd, look." Hiera grabbed his arm and pointed to the second-floor balcony of a wooden house across the street.

A tiny dwarf child stood on the balcony. Flames licked out the doorway behind him. In a moment the whole building would collapse. The other dwarves watched in horror.

"My little boy!" one of them screamed.

Mudd's gaze swept the street, looking for some way to get up to the balcony.

"Don't even think of going into that house," Hiera said. "You'd be dead before you reached the stairs."

Mudd pulled away from her grasp and drew his sword.

"What are you doing?" she cried again. "You can't fight fire with a sword!"

Ignoring her, Mudd raced to the light pole at the side of the street. Judging the distance and the angle to the burning house, Mudd chopped at the base of the thick wooden pole with his sword. A sliver of wood chipped away, then a second.

"Here, lad." A burley dwarf pressed an axe into his hands.

Mudd hefted the axe, getting a feel for the weapon to make sure he hit the pole just right before he swung. The dwarf boy's cry for help turned into a scream.

Mudd slammed the axe into the pole. Wood creaked. The pole tipped, then fell, crashing against the balcony. Mudd dropped the axe and ran up the pole to the burning house. He snatched the child from balcony and raced back toward the ground.

The house collapsed before he was halfway down. Wood thundered upon wood and roaring fire. The pole vanished from beneath his feet.

Mudd wrapped his arms around the child and tucked into a roll as he hit the ground. He came to his feet, breathless, and set the child down.

The dwarves crowded around, patting Mudd on the back and cheering. The mother swooped her toddler up, hugging him and kissing his cheek.

Mudd looked from the child to Stonefist Drakecutter. A dwarf cleric knelt beside the old dwarf, working feverishly to keep him alive. Stonefist's body was so burned the healer might not be able to save him. The dwarves muttered and shook their heads.

Mudd gripped the parchment in his pocket. Stonefist had to live. Mudd needed him to look at Shemnara's drawing.

Mudd tore his gaze away from them and stared into the collapsed house. The fire still raged, snapping and smoking. Its heat licked Mudd's cheeks. He stepped closer to the fire, thinking of Hector.

Hiera pulled him away from the burning house. "You're hurt, Mudd. Come over and let the healer look at you."

Mudd shook Hiera off and strode to where the cleric and Greenthumb knelt next to Stonefist.

"Can you save him, Thakil?" Greenthumb asked the healer.

The healer, a cleric of Mishakal, clutched the goddess's holy emblem in his hands. "It will take a miracle." He bowed his head again in prayer, pleading to Mishakal for Stonefist's life.

Mudd waited in silence, fingering the parchment.

The healer flinched, then looked straight at Greenthumb. "Your father made a pact with Reorx. Mishakal can't interfere. Whether he lives or dies depends on what becomes of his axe."

"It's gone," Greenthumb said through gritted teeth. "Stolen by the dragon, I think."

A look of resignation spread across Thakil's face. "Then the best I can do is make him comfortable until his soul passes from this world."

Mudd pulled his hand from the parchment in his pocket, disappointed.

Greenthumb jumped to his feet. "What if I find the axe and bring it back?"

Thakil gaped. "You're going to hunt a red dragon?"

"Yes, if that's what it takes to save my father." Greenthumb stared at the mountains where the dragon had gone.

"You'd better do it quickly, then," the healer said. "Stonefist doesn't have much time."

Chapter Nine

At the healer's urging, the other dwarves carefully lifted the burned Stonefist and carried him into the Drakecutters' house. Smoke still filled the street. Mudd put his arm over his mouth and coughed. His lungs felt like they were on fire. He staggered away. Each step brought stinging pain from his burned feet.

"What are you doing?" Hiera cried. "We can't leave until the cleric has a look at you. You're in no condition to move."

Mudd waved a dismissive hand. "The healer has his own people to worry about. A lot of dwarves are in worse shape than I am." He laughed. "I'll be fine."

"Mudd, please." She caught his arm and called to the dwarves who were throwing buckets of water on the burning buildings.

Mudd's stomach twisted, and he tried to quiet Hiera. He just wanted to get away from the smoke and flames and be alone for a while.

"Dear boy, where are you going?" The mother of the dwarf

child he'd saved rushed over to him. Her brown dress was covered with soot. She wrapped a thick arm around Mudd's waist and hauled him back toward the Drakecutter house.

Mudd tried to protest, but for some reason his eyesight went fuzzy and his legs wouldn't work anymore.

Mudd flinched as the dwarf cleric rubbed salve on the bottoms of his burned feet. He sat on a chair in the Drakecutter kitchen, where they'd taken him after he collapsed in the street.

"Hold still," Hiera admonished.

"Easy for you to say," Mudd muttered through gritted teeth.

The burning building had melted his boots to his feet, and chunks of skin had peeled off when the healer removed them.

While Thakil tended Mudd's burns, Greenthumb raced around the kitchen, shoving supplies into a pack and cursing the red dragon under his breath. Mudd's stomach grumbled. He hoped the dwarf didn't clear out the whole larder before setting out after the dragon.

A deep frown creased Hiera's face.

Mudd gave her a jaunty smile. "I'm all right, Hiera." He immediately belied his confidence when he yelped in pain. He tried to pull his feet away as Thakil wrapped a bandage around the burns.

"Hold still," the healer said.

Hiera rolled her eyes. I'm sure you'll be fine, Mudd, but what are we going to do now? If Stonefist can't tell us where to find that door, how will we get the pendant and save Shemnara?"

Greenthumb stopped with a half of a smoked ham in his hand, ready to shove it into his bag. "What door? Isn't Shemnara the seer from Potter's Mill? I've heard of her."

Hiera put her hands on her hips. "Yes, Shemnara is our seer, and she's been kidnapped by the dragon."

"The same dragon who just burned Greenhollow to the ground? Why would the dragon take Shemnara?" Greenthumb put the ham on the table and raked his fingers through his already mussed beard. "Of course, I suppose I could ask the same of why she just burned Greenhollow. . . ."

"We don't know," Hiera said. "But she left a note telling us to—"

Mudd jumped to his feet, ignoring the sting of pain from the burns, and pressed his hand over Hiera's mouth.

The cleric exploded in exasperation. He chanted a quick prayer to Mishakal, asking for a blessing of healing for Mudd's feet. Then, muttering under his breath, he put away his salves and stalked out of the room.

"What's the matter with you?" Hiera asked, prying Mudd's hand from her mouth.

"Greenthumb's got his own problems to worry about." Mudd took Hiera's arm and dragged her into the living room, where two bare hooks over the fireplace showed the place an

57

axe once hung. "Hiera, you can't go around telling people about our quest. Not everyone here is your friend. We have to wait for Stonefist to wake up. He's the one who would know."

"The cleric said my father isn't likely to wake up anytime soon," Greenthumb said, stepping into the room. "Hiera said something about a stone door. I'm not my father, but perhaps I might help."

Mudd sighed. He had to admit the dwarf was right. "We're looking for a stone door with runes carved into it. A friend from home said there were lots of caves in this area, and that Master Drakecutter might know them well enough to point us in the right direction."

Greenthumb's shoulders slumped. "You're right. I can't help. My father doesn't let me wander the caves, here or anywhere else. But if you're looking for information, the best place to go is the Great Library of Palanthas."

The library, of course, Mudd thought, where Astinus the Chronicler kept the history of the world.

"Great idea," Hiera said. "If any place has information about the dragon pendant, the library will."

"Dragon pendant? What's that?" Greenthumb took a step toward them.

"Nothing," Mudd said.

"But it's so strange," Hiera said. "First the dragon comes to Potter's Mill and kidnaps Shemnara. Then she attacks Greenhollow and takes Stonefist's magic axe. They must be connected somehow."

"Perhaps they are." Greenthumb set down his overstuffed pack. "Tell me what you know."

"No," Mudd said. "It's none of your affair."

Hiera slapped his arm. Before Mudd could stop her, she started telling Greenthumb all about the silver dragon, the pendant, and the tests that were supposed to guard the door to it.

While she talked, Mudd retreated to the kitchen, grabbed the ham off the table, and helped himself to a bite. He leaned back in a chair, glad to get off his stinging feet. Smoke from the burning village hung heavy in the air, even inside the snug stone home. But the succulent meat filled his stomach and settled his nerves.

"You should come with us to Palanthas." Hiera's high-pitched voice jerked him upright in his chair.

"Now, Hiera," Mudd called through the doorway to the living room. "Greenthumb is going after the red dragon to get his father's axe. He doesn't have time to come with us to Palanthas."

Greenthumb charged into the kitchen and grabbed the front of Mudd's shirt, growling. "The name's Drakecutter. Call me Greenthumb again and I'll chop you to kindling."

"But . . . that's what your father called you," Mudd spluttered.

"My father named me Greenthumb because he wants me to be a farmer. But I'm not a farmer. I'm a warrior." Greenthumb shook Mudd, then released him and stepped back. "The name is Drakecutter, and don't you forget it. My father is dying, and the only way I can save him is to get back his axe."

Greenthumb—no, Drakecutter—calmed his breathing a little and continued. "Hiera's right. I could search for months up in those mountains for the dragon's lair. But I don't have months. If we work together we could find the dragon pendant quickly and summon the silver dragon. We can ask her to get both Shemnara and the axe."

Mudd swallowed a bite of meat and put the ham down. "We can ask her?" He didn't like how quickly the younger Drakecutter had included himself in their quest.

"Yes, we can ask her," Drakecutter said.

Mudd stood, wincing just a little. His feet were still tender, but they no longer hurt. "For all you know it will take us longer to find the pendant than to search for the dragon's lair. Why don't we split up? You go search for the dragon, and Hiera and I will go to Palanthas."

Drakecutter huffed, picked up his pack, and walked to the door. "Thanks for saving my father," he said in a low voice. "That took a lot of courage."

"Or sheer idiocy," Hiera said. "Something like what he's doing now." Hiera wrapped her arms around Drakecutter in a tight hug. "Be careful," she whispered.

She released him, and her eyes sparkled with a clever gleam. "You might as well start your search for the dragon in the mountains between here and Palanthas."

Drakecutter gave Hiera a grim smile and stomped out of the house.

Mudd sank back into the chair, feeling wretched for some odd reason.

Kirak climbed off Redclaw's back and flung the axe into the dragon's horde. It clattered against the other treasure and settled at the base of a thick wooden chest.

Before he could take a step, he doubled over and emptied the contents of his stomach on the floor. Fortunately he'd eaten so little in the last week it didn't make much mess.

Redclaw laughed at him and blew a wisp of flame at his back that ignited his shirt. "You always were too softhearted."

As Kirak beat the fire out, he glared at Redclaw. "You didn't have to kill Stonefist." During their long flight back to the lair, Redclaw had bragged about smashing the old dwarf into the fire and letting him burn.

Redclaw snorted. "Yes, I did have to dispose of Stonefist. Otherwise he would come for his axe himself. But with him out of the way, Greenthumb is sure to join Mudd in his quest for the pendant."

"But Stonefist was nice to me when I stopped in Greenhollow while searching for the pendant," Kirak whispered to himself.

Redclaw's keen ears picked up his whisper. "Stonefist was nice to you," she mimicked. "Stonefist was a fool to tell a stranger about his axe—an axe you can use to kill the silver dragon after you summon her."

Redclaw turned her scaly back on him and slithered to the far reaches of her lair.

"The only foolish thing was letting you find out about it," Kirak muttered as soon as she was out of hearing range.

He shuddered. After Redclaw had captured him, she'd sifted through his mind with merciless cruelty, flaying away all pretense to discover his true identity. She'd torn the knowledge of the dragon pendant and the magic axe from his memories as well, though he battled with all his will to stop her. Then she'd used his own thoughts to come up with the plan she'd forced on him.

Kirak moaned. His life was a curse to himself and everyone he came in contact with. He was a vile creature, born of darkness. As long as he lived, more people would die—Mudd and Greenthumb for sure, and perhaps many others.

"I wish I'd never been born," he cried.

"Kirak." Shemnara's soft voice froze him.

She stood in the doorway of her alcove, her face calm, and her gaze soothing despite the heavy manacle that still clung to her wrist. "Your life is not hopeless."

"I see no hope." Kirak's ragged voice echoed around the chamber.

"You are not a seer," Shemnara said. "You can't see the future. You believe you are doomed based on what you think is going to happen. But there is no truth in your assumption—the future may play out in many different ways. As long as you live and breathe, there is hope for a better tomorrow."

Kirak stared into her wrinkled old face. A flicker of hope lit in him. "You have seen my future? Was there more to your vision that you didn't tell me?"

"I have seen what you are, and I know what you can be," Shemnara said. "Embrace loyalty and friendship. They are stronger than a dragon's magic."

Kirak grimaced and walked to the mouth of the cave. He stared down across the rugged mountains toward Greenhollow. Loyalty and friendship could just as easily turn into betrayal.

CHAPTER TEN

iera waited for the young Drakecutter to leave before rounding on Mudd. "Of all the stubborn, obnoxious, arrogant brothers, I had to get you. We could have used Drakecutter's help."

"We can handle this on our own," Mudd answered. His face grew hot, and he glared at his sister.

"Oh come on," Hiera said. "Even the great adventurers in stories don't go off on their own. They take all kinds of people to help them."

"Shemnara's note said I was supposed to seek the silver dragon. If she'd meant for you or anyone else to come with me, she would have mentioned them, don't you think?"

Hiera put her hands on her hips, reminding Mudd of his mother. "I'm sure she wanted others to help. There just wasn't time for her to write it."

"No," Mudd said, getting up. "We go to Palanthas on our own, tonight."

A worried look crossed Hiera's face. "The cleric told me you should stay off your feet until morning." She took Mudd's hand. "Come on. Greenthumb—I mean Drakecutter—said there's a bed you can use in the other room. We're welcome to stay as long as we want."

Mudd tried to argue, but his body rebelled. He felt faint and tired. His feet throbbed as Hiera led him into the bedroom and forced him to lie down.

He woke early the next morning while stars still glimmered in the sky. The smell of smoke hung in the air—not the scent of a good clean pine fire crackling in the fireplace, but the choking smell of burned thatch, rugs, and clothes—the horrifying aftermath of the red dragon's devastation.

Mudd gagged and crept out of bed to the window. The air outside smelled worse, and he slammed the window shut, a little too loud. He whirled around, wondering where Hiera was and if he'd wakened her.

"Who's there?" a gruff but feeble voice called from the next room. "Greenthumb, is that you?"

Mudd hesitated. It had to be Stonefist, the master of the house.

"Greenthumb?" the dwarf's voice grew softer and held a hint of desperation.

Mudd slipped out of his room and into the next one. A dwindling candle burned on the table beside the bed, showing the old dwarf tucked in bed, his face and body bandaged. Only his eyes were visible through the white cloth.

"You're not Greenthumb," the dwarf said. He coughed, a painful wracking cough that didn't subside for a few minutes.

"No, Master Drakecutter," Mudd said, stepping over to the bed.

"Well, where is he?" the dwarf asked sourly.

Mudd glanced out the window at the mountains that loomed over the village. He wondered if he should tell Stonefist that his son had gone hunting a red dragon on his own. It was foolish. Mudd should never have allowed him to go off like that.

"Answer me, boy. You're in my house. Show a bit of respect," Stonefist barked.

"He's gone after the red dragon," Mudd said, wincing.

"He what? If he took my axe, I'll tan his hide. Hunting a red dragon. That's preposterous. Even Greenthumb wouldn't be that foolish." Stonefist pounded his bandaged fists against the blankets.

Mudd took a step back. The dwarf was intimidating enough all wrapped in bandages. He'd hate to see Stonefist angry on a good day. He licked his lips and tried to explain. "Greenthumb didn't take your axe. The dragon stole it. The cleric said Greenthumb had to get it back or you would die."

Stonefist's eyes widened, and he slumped against the pillow. "No. . . . It can't be. Gone?"

"I'm afraid so," Mudd said.

The fire seeped out of Stonecutter's eyes. "Who are you?"

"My name is Mudd. I'm from Potter's Mill over on the other side of the pass. I pulled you out of the fire." Mudd fumbled in his pocket for Shemnara's drawing. He held it out. "I traveled here to seek you, wondering if you'd ever seen a door like this."

Stonefist squinted at the drawing. "Those don't look like any runes I've ever seen before."

"But the stonework? It's so good, and it's underground. I thought maybe you—"

"No. I'm a hill dwarf, boy. Hill dwarves don't live underground." Pride and some long-standing resentment mixed in Stonefist's voice.

"Oh." Mudd shoved the parchment back in his pocket. "I'm sorry I bothered you." He turned to leave.

"Mudd." Stonefist reached out a bandaged hand. "Find my son, please. Don't let him go after the red dragon. She'll kill him. He should go to Palanthas and call on the Solamnic Knights for help."

Mudd hesitated. Stonefist was right. If Greenthumb fought the red dragon, he'd be killed.

Stonefist closed his eyes and moaned, "My son, my son. Reorx, spare him. The pledge was mine, not his."

Mudd touched the old dwarf's bandaged arm. "Don't worry, I'll find him and take him with me to Palanthas. No harm will come to him."

Stonefist's eyes remained closed, his breathing ragged. He gave no sign that he'd heard Mudd's promise.

Mudd backed out of the room and ran into Hiera.

She stood shivering in the hall in a pale pink nightdress, her hair in tangled waves around her shoulders. It was as if the night had transformed her from the confident ranger back into the fragile little sister he'd always known.

"How is he?" Hiera whispered.

"Not good," Mudd said, putting an arm around her shoulders. "He made me promise we'd take Greenthumb with us."

Hiera's eyes lit up with joy, and she hugged him. "I'm so glad. But you better not call him Greenthumb to his face."

"Right. I guess we better go now and hope he hasn't traveled too far for us to catch him. Do you think you can pick up his trail?" Mudd asked.

"Sure. I'll go get dressed." Hiera darted down the hall and vanished into another room.

Mudd went in search of his pack and weapons. He found them in the cozy living room on a sturdy dwarf chair next to the fireplace. A new pair of boots stood next to his pack. They were crafted from gray suede, with black scrollwork stretching up the sides. The soles were sturdy for hiking, but with an extra cushion inside to pad his feet. Mudd sat on a chair and pulled them on over his bandages. They fit perfectly.

Hiera walked into the room, dressed for travel. The delicate girl was gone, replaced by a strong ranger.

"Where did these come from?" Mudd asked, admiring the boots.

"The mother of the child you saved from the balcony is a cobbler and wanted to do something to thank you," Hiera said. "The leather to make them was all she could salvage from her shop. The dwarves have almost nothing left, but they filled our packs with food and replaced your boots and burned cloak. You're their hero."

She grinned at him and headed for the front door.

Mudd frowned. He didn't feel like a hero, sending Greenthumb off to fight the dragon alone. He slung his pack on his back, grabbed his weapons, and followed Hiera out into the chilly morning.

CHAPTER ELEVEN

"This way," Hiera said. She led Mudd out of the village and across a flat area where the dwarves slept in makeshift tents. A few of the dwarf women were already up, lighting fires to prepare a scant morning meal with whatever they had salvaged from their burned homes.

"Looks like Drakecutter is following the direct path the dragon took away from here," Hiera said.

She sprinted away from Mudd. He tried to follow, but the extra pressure of running hurt his tender feet. He winced and dropped back to a walk.

"Oh you poor boy," one of the dwarf women said, patting him on the back.

"I'm all right, really," Mudd said. He smiled at her and tried to move on, but others pressed around him, babbling.

"Such courage."

"And so young."

"Are you a knight?"

"Thank you. No," Mudd said, pushing past them. Flushing

with embarrassment, he hurried away. When he caught up to Hiera at the edge of a field, she reached her arm out to stop him.

"What?" Mudd asked. He moved back and stared at the ground Hiera indicated.

The newly plowed soil was a churned-up mess. Deep claw marks gouged the ground.

Hiera knelt and touched the dirt with her finger, then got up and retraced her steps. She shook her head. "It's hard to tell. The dwarves have been running all over this field since the dragon left."

"Tell what?" Mudd asked. "Even I can see the dragon landed here."

Hiera rolled her eyes. "The dragon never went into Drakecutter's home. That means she must have sent some smaller creature in to get the axe, then picked it up here before she left. Evil dragons aren't the only beings that serve the Dark Queen."

Mudd stared harder at the messy ground. "Like in Potter's Mill? You think the dragon's got a draconian with her?"

Hiera frowned. "Set-ai said whoever took Shemnara was carrying a pair of draconian swords, but there were no draconian tracks in Potter's Mill." Hiera shook her head. "I don't see any draconian tracks here either."

"How would you know what draconian tracks look like?" Mudd asked.

"Set-ai drew one in the dirt for me before I left." Hiera pointed to a few places on the ground. "I can tell your footprints, mine, Drakecutter's, and several other dwarves', but I don't see anything that looks like a draconian track." She put her hands on her hips and glared at the dirt.

Dawn's pale light illuminated the horizon. Mudd shivered in the chilly morning air. "All right. It wasn't a draconian. What was it?"

"Look at this," Hiera said, going back to the place next to the dragon prints that she had touched.

Mudd knelt and stared at the ground where she pointed. Gradually he made out the shape of a foot, barely visible on the ground. "Whoever made it must not weigh very much. You sure that isn't your own footprint?" he asked.

Hiera rolled her eyes and stepped next to the other print. Her foot left behind a much narrower mark, a couple of inches smaller than the print Hiera studied.

"Wow, you have little feet," Mudd said, grinning at her. "Maybe it was a young dwarf."

Hiera frowned, her forehead puckered in concentration. "No, dwarf feet are broader, even the young ones'. Mudd, this is a human footprint, made by someone your age. A boy, probably. Taller than you, but not much heavier."

"I'm getting bigger." Mudd straightened and adjusted his pack. "I suppose you're right about the footprint, though. We'd better hurry and find Drakecutter before the dragon or her human helper finds him first."

Hiera hesitated. "I've been thinking about something Set-ai told us about the draconians. Remember, he said that a sivak draconian can take the form of someone it's killed. If it killed a human, it could move about in disguise."

Mudd grimaced. "That makes sense. It would be pretty easy to spot and kill otherwise."

A sliver of worry niggled its way into him. With Hiera ready to trust everyone they ran into, Mudd didn't like the odds of getting a knife in the back like Set-ai had described.

If the dragon's ally were a draconian, and it found Drakecutter and killed him before Mudd and Hiera got to him, they would never know the difference until it was too late. Mudd vowed to keep a close eye on the dwarf when they found him.

Mudd and Hiera left the field and followed the young Drakecutter's tracks up into the Vingaard Mountains. They pressed forward until around noon, when the trail led straight up a steep slope to a wall of rock.

Mudd slumped to the ground and fished in his pack for something to eat.

Hiera shook her head in frustration. "What was he thinking? Wasn't he watching where he was going? Of course a dwarf can't fly straight up the side of the mountain like a dragon can."

"It was dark," Mudd said. He bit into a soft loaf of bread provided by the dwarves. "He probably didn't see this until he got here."

"Don't talk with your mouth full, Mudd. That's disgusting," Hiera chided.

Mudd grinned at her and stuck out his bread-covered tongue.

She turned her back on him and studied the ground for a while. "He went this way, skirting the cliff face. Come on, let's go. I want to catch him before nightfall."

Mudd grimaced and got to his feet. "Don't you know it's bad luck to go adventuring on an empty stomach?"

"You just made that up," Hiera said. She followed Drakecutter's trail to a break in the cliff, where a landslide provided a path farther up the mountain.

Up they went, and up again, to where the mountain leveled off on a desolate rocky shoulder. Drakecutter's footprints were harder to make out against the gritty rocks, and Hiera had to crisscross back and forth to find the way.

Daylight had started to dim when they came to another dead end at the top of a sheer cliff, looking down. One step off the edge and a person would fall hundreds of feet.

Mudd squinted into the crimson sunset. A brown lump lay unmoving on the ground at the base of the cliff.

Hiera gasped and put her hand to her mouth. "Oh no, Mudd. Do you think that's him? He would have reached this cliff during daylight. He couldn't have fallen."

Mudd knelt and leaned over the edge. "Drakecutter!" he yelled. His voice echoed between the mountain peaks. The lump of cloth and leather below didn't respond.

"Drakecutter!" Hiera screamed. "Drakecutter!"

"Oh, hello," a gruff voice spoke from behind them. "It's you, is it? Did you decide to skip Palanthas and just hunt the dragon yourself?"

Hiera whirled around, and Mudd jumped to his feet.

The burly young dwarf stood there stretching his thick, muscled arms over his head. "Sorry I didn't see you come up. I decided to take a little rest and fell asleep for a bit."

"Oh, Drakecutter," Hiera cried. She hugged him, and he flushed crimson. "We thought you were dead. There's something down there." She pointed over the side of the cliff.

Drakecutter shook his head ruefully. "It's my pack. I was looking over the edge and dropped it."

Mudd took a deep breath and stepped away from the cliff. His hand strayed to his sword hilt. In truth, the dwarf no longer had a pack. But it could just as easily be a convenient lie. The real Drakecutter could be dead at the bottom of the cliff and a sivak draconian standing before them. Mudd wished he knew enough about the dwarf to ask a question that only the real Drakecutter could answer.

"Don't worry," Hiera said. "Mudd has plenty of food in his pack, and even if he eats it all today, I can always hunt us up something to eat later. But we're not going after the red dragon. We've come to convince you to go to Palanthas with us to find out more about the silver dragon pendant."

"I thought he didn't want me along," Drakecutter said, stabbing a thick finger at Mudd.

Mudd hadn't, and now he really didn't, but it was too late to back out.

"It's all right," Hiera said. "Mudd talked to your father. You're coming with us."

"You talked to my father? He's awake?" Drakecutter stepped toward Mudd.

"He regained consciousness briefly," Mudd explained. "He wants you to go to Palanthas and ask the knights to fight the dragon. I didn't have the chance to tell him about the pendant. But he didn't know where the stone door was, so we're going to the Great Library like you suggested."

Drakecutter groaned and kicked at the ground. "My father will never let me become the great warrior I was meant to be. I can kill the dragon. I know I can."

"But not without the axe," Hiera said, grabbing hold of Drakecutter's hand. "Help us find the pendant. You can ask the silver dragon to get the axe back. *Then* you can kill the red dragon."

Drakecutter hesitated, then nodded. "All right. I'll come with you."

Mudd flinched. His sister might be holding a draconian's hand. Or not. It could really be Drakecutter. "This is a lousy place to camp," he said. "We'll freeze to death up here after nightfall. Let's find a way down before it gets too dark."

He let Hiera and Drakecutter go in front and kept his hand on his sword. If Drakecutter did anything funny, he'd strike first.

CHAPTER TWELVE

True dark had settled by the time Mudd, Hiera, and Drakecutter got off the high shoulder and into a more sheltered glen. Mudd slumped to the ground and eased his boots off. From the way his feet throbbed, he feared the bandages would be soaked with blood. It surprised him when he unwound them to find new, pink skin beneath.

A campfire crackled to life, and Mudd looked up to see the dwarf coaxing it into a roaring flame.

"Stop," Mudd said. "You have to keep the fire small so it won't be seen by enemies."

"What enemies?" Drakecutter grunted and shoved another log on the blaze.

"The dragon, for one," Mudd said. The heat stung his feet, and he inched away from the fire.

"I hope she does see it," Drakecutter growled. "Come here, you big ugly beast," he yelled into the darkness. "You can't hide forever."

Mudd groaned.

Hiera reached out and stopped Drakecutter from adding yet another piece of wood to the fire. "We're not hunting the dragon, remember? We're going to Palanthas."

"Besides," Mudd said, rising and drawing his sword. "The dragon isn't our only enemy. There may be a sivak draconian working with her. But I imagine he'd be a lot easier to kill."

Drakecutter dropped the log and pulled out a broad-bladed dagger. "A sivak? You mean a shapechanger?"

"Yes," Hiera said. "The dragon couldn't have taken the axe from your house without demolishing everything. She has someone working with her, either a human or a sivak in human form. We saw the draconian's footprints."

Mudd gripped his sword and eased into a fighting stance. "Of course it can take any form it wants by simply killing the person it needs to look like." He tensed for an attack.

Drakecutter frowned and stared off into the forest. "We'd better take turns keeping watch at night then. I hate draconians. My father told me about fighting them. Evil spawn of the Dark Queen. I'd like to stick my knife into a few."

Mudd frowned. Drakecutter didn't act like Mudd imagined a draconian would. Mudd couldn't have come out more clearly in accusing it, but Drakecutter hadn't responded like a draconian in disguise.

Hiera cleared her throat. "Drakecutter, you weren't planning on fighting the dragon with that dagger, were you?"

Drakecutter looked down at his hand. The weapon he held was a good sturdy dagger, thick enough that it wouldn't break easily, and sharp enough to be effective against anything but plate mail . . . or dragon scales.

Drakecutter flushed. "Of course not. If you have to know, I planned to sneak into her lair and get my father's axe. Then kill her. No sense hefting any other axe up the mountain since it would be as useless as this dagger against the dragon." He put the dagger away. "Now, how about some food and some sleep? Mudd seems ready to take the first watch."

Hiera and Drakecutter sat down to eat. Mudd kept his sword out and ready until he couldn't stand the smell of toasted bread and cheese any longer. Then he set it aside and gobbled a bit of food.

He slept little that night, taking first watch, then watching Drakecutter keep second watch. Hiera got up for the third watch. Mudd waited for Drakecutter to fall into deep snores before rising and padding to where she stood away from the smoldering remains of the fire.

"Hiera," Mudd said.

She started and turned to him with her knives drawn. "You're supposed to be asleep, Mudd. The healer told me you'll need plenty of rest for your body to recover."

"I'll sleep now, but I want you to keep an eye on Drakecutter." Mudd was tired. It had been a struggle to stay awake so far.

"Drakecutter? Why?" Hiera glanced at the sleeping dwarf.

"Just in case what we saw at the bottom of the cliff wasn't his pack," Mudd said.

"What else would it be?" Hiera asked.

Mudd didn't want to tell her that Drakecutter might be dead, but she had to know for her own safety. In a whisper he explained to her his theory about a sivak taking Drakecutter's form.

Hiera stood silent, fingering her knives. When he finished, she pivoted so she could see Drakecutter as well as the dark forest beyond their camp. "You haven't slept all night, have you?" she asked.

Mudd shook his head.

"It's a long road to Palanthas," Hiera said, her face grim in the red light of the glowing coals. "I suggest you and I keep our own watch schedule, half the night each."

Mudd nodded, surprised she'd accepted his theory without argument. He crawled onto his bedroll and pulled the blanket over him. A last glance at his sister showed her cheeks wet with tears.

CHAPTER THIRTEEN

The next morning they set out for Palanthas. Worried what might happen to Shemnara during the time it took them to reach the city, Mudd kept them moving at a fast pace.

They skirted the lower foothills for three days until they came to the road that led up into Westgate Pass. An imposing fortress blocked their way with an immense tower jutting up into the sky.

"The High Clerist's Tower," Drakecutter said, staring at the structure with bright eyes. "It's magnificent. Did you know this was where one of the most famous battles of the war was fought?"

"Set-ai talked about it some," Hiera said.

Mudd's heart pounded. He didn't care what battles might have been fought here. That tower looked like a fun place to explore. He could spend days searching all its halls and chambers. He crushed the thought before it could go too far. They couldn't waste time here.

Mudd hefted his pack and strode up the road that led

through a smaller section of the complex on the right. Drakecutter hesitated and then followed, along with Hiera. The way dropped them onto the Knight's High Road that led up into the mountains. Tall peaks rose on either side of them. Here, spring had come later—the trees were just starting to bud, and a cold wind blew down the pass.

Mudd wrapped his cloak around him, put his head down into the wind, and hurried on. They spoke little and only stopped to rest a few times during the day. Even with their quick pace, there was still no sign of Palanthas by the time the sky darkened. Mudd kept going. He worried that Hiera might be tiring, but she never protested.

By the time stars appeared above them, Drakecutter stamped to a stop in the middle of the road. "It's cold, and I'm hungry. We'd better light a fire and camp for the night."

Mudd started to protest, but his stomach rumbled so loudly that Hiera laughed.

"One more night, Mudd. I'm sure we'll get there tomorrow," she said, stepping off the road into stand of pine trees. She let her pack drop and disappeared into the brush with her bow in hand.

While she was hunting, Mudd gathered dry sticks and lit a fire. Drakecutter squatted down beside him and held his hands up to the flames. There wasn't much left in Mudd's pack except for a couple of apples. He pulled them out and frowned at the wrinkled and bruised skin.

"Here. Those will be better roasted," Drakecutter said. He

took one of the apples from Mudd and speared it on a stick.

Mudd laughed. "I suppose you're right. And if Hiera doesn't catch anything, this may be all we get." Mudd put the second apple on the stick and held it over the fire. The juice popped and sizzled, making Mudd's mouth water.

He didn't suppose the apple would taste as good as a home-cooked meal, but it might take the edge off his hunger. If Hector were with him now, he'd probably invent some machine that would turn the apples over the fire so Mudd's fingers wouldn't get so hot.

At the thought of Hector, Mudd's appetite vanished. He handed his stick to Drakecutter and walked away from the fire. At the edge of the light he stopped and scanned the forest for any sign of Hiera.

"You don't like me much, do you?" Drakecutter huffed. "Can't see any reason for it."

Mudd stared at the dwarf. Though Drakecutter was shorter, his heavy body outweighed Mudd's. He sat by the fire with his braided beard tucked into his belt to keep it from the flames. Mudd searched his dark eyes for any sign of a draconian hidden inside. If there were, it had never once slipped from pretending to be the dwarf.

Other than the lost pack, Mudd had no cause to think Drakecutter meant him any harm. Still, Mudd's gut screamed for him to stay away from the dwarf. Mudd swallowed a lump in his throat.

Hiera stepped into the firelight carrying a couple of dead

rabbits by the hind legs. "Roast apples. Smells good."

Drakecutter handed her the one that had been Mudd's.

Ignoring them, Mudd sat with his back to a tree trunk and pulled out a bundle of black cloth from a hidden pocket in his shirt. He eased the cloth back to reveal a set of slender metal rods and other odd-shaped instruments. With these he could pick any lock. While Hiera had practiced swordsmanship and archery with Set-ai, Mudd had spent his time collecting and honing his skills with these tiny tools.

He picked up each one, ran his fingers over the smooth metal, and set it down again, until Hiera finished cooking the rabbits. By then his appetite had returned, and he shoved the meat into his mouth as soon as it was cool enough to eat.

Mudd turned a bend in the road and halted. Hiera gasped.

Sunlight glittered off a white city in the valley below. Magnificent spires reached to the sky. Broad roads spread out from the center like spokes of a wheel.

Mudd blinked. "I knew Palanthas was big, but that's just impossible."

"The whole of Potter's Mill wouldn't even take up one block," Hiera said. "Look at all those people."

Mudd grinned. So many houses and shops, mansions, and towers. His heart pounded. "Come on," he cried and hurried down the steep switchbacks toward the city below. His pack thumped against his back with each rushed step.

Drakecutter grunted and jogged to keep up with him.

Before they reached the city, they came to a stone gatehouse built across the road. To either side of it, steep cliffs stopped any passage except through the gate.

A pair of young knights stood in the gateway, blocking the path with crossed polearms.

"State your business," they commanded.

Before Mudd could speak, Hiera stepped forward. "There's a red dragon terrorizing the villages in the southern Vingaard Mountains. It burned our village, and the dwarf's. We've come to seek your aid."

The knights stiffened. "A red, you say?" the taller of the two asked.

"Yes, a big one." Hiera somehow managed to look feminine even in her ranger clothes and carrying her weapons. Mudd couldn't be sure, but it looked like she might be flirting with the tall knight.

"Don't worry," the knight said. "We'll take care of it." He nodded to his companion and both knights lifted their polearms out of the way and smiled at Hiera.

Drakecutter chuckled. "Your sister's as beautiful as they come, I suppose. At least it seems the young knights thinks so."

Mudd frowned. His little sister?

"There is a nice inn close to the Old City Wall called

Paladine's Prize," the tall knight said. "It's comfortable and not too pricey."

"Yes," the other knight agreed. "And if you stay there, we will be able to find you to learn more about your troubles. Will you leave us your names?"

Hiera gave them both a winsome smile. "Thank you, sirs. You are kind." She told them her name and the names of her companions, then walked past, motioning for Mudd and Drakecutter to follow.

CHAPTER FOURTEEN

Mudd strode into Palanthas with Hiera and Drakecutter beside him. A broad thoroughfare led them toward the heart of the city. Trees with golden leaves in full spring splendor lined the street. Stately white buildings rose in pristine glory on either side. A farmer with a cart of radishes trundled past, the wheels clacking against the flagstones.

In front of a shop on the left, a row of game hens turned on a spit over an open fire pit. The shop owner toasted bread and cheese while his son called out to passersby. The boy's shrill cries promised a succulent feast to the throngs of chattering women who pressed around Mudd, hurrying from one shop to another.

Mudd's stomach grumbled.

Hiera slapped his arm. "We're entering the Jewel of Solamnia, and all you can think about is food?"

A cart of iron ore trundled along the side of the road, pulled by a pair of heavy draft horses.

"Look at that," Drakecutter said, tugging at his beard.

"Do you have any idea how much steel that could make? Oh, this city." He spread his hands in appreciation, lagging behind Hiera and Mudd. "The stonework. The craftsmanship. I should have come to Palanthas long ago. And this, the dwarves built for humans. What I wouldn't give to see a real dwarf city like Thorbardin."

"Why don't you?" Hiera asked.

Drakecutter flushed. "Hill dwarves aren't exactly welcome underground. Whole wars have been fought over it." He paused as two children raced in front of him and disappeared into a candy shop.

"Why not build your own underground cities?" Hiera asked.

Drakecutter growled something under his breath that sounded suspiciously like a long string of swear words.

Mudd laughed.

"Oh look," Hiera said. A shimmering white tower rose up on either side of the street in front of them, and a thick wall stretched off around the inner city. Between the towers a gateway arched over the road.

"That must be the Old City Wall," Mudd said. "I suppose the inn has to be close, probably on the other side of the gate."

Mudd stared up at the towers as he passed between them, wondering how he might get inside and climb to the top. Solamnic locks were easy enough to open. His hand pressed against the small bundle in his shirt. What fun he'd have sneaking in. Except . . . . He shook his head. Exploring the gate towers wouldn't help him get Shemnara back.

Just beyond the gate, hundreds of merchant stalls filled a broad square. Awnings of red, gold, and blue lit the space with color and flapped in the evening breeze. Sizzling pig and beef hung roasting over an open fire in the center of the square.

"We should go on straight to the inn," Mudd said even as his feet carried him off the road and into the square. "After we arrange a room, we can visit the library."

"It can't hurt to look just for a minute." Hiera's eyes glittered as she stared at the market. "Set-ai gave me some steel before I left, and when are we ever going to get a chance like this again?"

She hurried over to a stall that flowed with ribbons, silk, and jewelry.

Drakecutter shook his head. "Better settle in for a wait, Mudd. Looks like we could be here a while."

"Right." Mudd watched a juggler make his way toward him. Colored balls blurred in a circle over the juggler's head.

When the juggler came even with him, Mudd snatched three of the balls from the air and sent them spinning above his own head.

The juggler stopped in surprise, and the rest of the balls would have fallen to the ground, except Mudd caught them and flipped them into the air.

"Have you ever tried it with knives?" Mudd asked. "I've been meaning to, but I've never had the chance."

"Sure, I do knives, torches, all that stuff." The juggler pulled the spinning balls back to his own hand and stepped away.

Mudd grinned and dropped a copper coin into the metal cup fastened on the juggler's belt.

The click of gears and squeal of metal moving against metal caught Mudd's attention. Across the way, two gnomes in greasy leather aprons stood beside a stand that displayed a wondrous array of mechanical inventions.

Mudd abandoned the juggler and raced over to stare at a mechanical bear that bobbed and danced. Beside it, a little toy gnome ratcheted up a ladder to a red moon on a stand above.

"Hector would have loved this," Mudd said, staring in wonder.

One of the gnomes leaned forward. "You like it? You want to buy it for Hector? Is he your little brother, perhaps?"

"No. Hector was my friend," Mudd said. "A gnome. His father is Bloody Bob. Perhaps you've heard of him?"

"Sure, we know Bloody Bob," the first gnome said. Their heads nodded in unison, their curly white hair bouncing around their lined faces.

"I'm Wig and this is my brother Twig," one said. "We live not far from him in Haggersmoore." Wig gave Mudd a wide smile that made his fat nose look even fatter. "Bloody Bob's son died on a grand adventure. Is that the Hector you mean?"

Mudd clenched his fists. "You don't have to look so happy about it."

"We meant no offense," Twig said, edging away from Mudd. "Hector's death restored honor to his family and proved he and his father were some of the greatest gnomes in Haggersmoore!"

Wig motioned to the devices on the table. "You'd like to purchase something, perhaps?"

Mudd swallowed, unballed his fists, and picked up a set of interlocked metal rings. He couldn't blame Wig and Twig for being proud of Hector.

"It's a puzzle game," Wig said. "The idea is to get the rings apa—"

Mudd slipped the rings apart and handed them to the gnome.

"Perhaps something a little more difficult," Twig said, reaching under the counter and bringing out another puzzle, more complicated than the last, with half a dozen metal strands.

Mudd took it and squinted at the tangled pieces.

"Let's see you get that one apart," Wig said. Both gnomes looked at him with eager anticipation. Mudd jiggled the pieces, twisted them around, and studied the puzzle from every direction, trying to see some pattern.

The gnomes laughed. "That ought to take you a while," Twig said. "For five pieces of copper, it's yours."

Mudd fished the money out of his coin bag and set it on the stand, then went back to fiddling with the puzzle.

Hiera walked up beside him. "All right. I'm finished. We should go find this inn before it gets dark."

"Sure," Mudd said. He followed her back to the street, where Drakecutter stood waiting for them.

"Well, lass, what did you buy?" Drakecutter asked.

Hiera held up a red lacquered box.

Mudd looked up from his puzzle. "What is it?"

Hiera unclasped the latch and took out a red comb. Then she unfolded the box so it lay flat in her hand, where Mudd could see that each panel of the box's interior was mirrored. Flat, Hiera could hold it up to see her reflection while she combed her hair.

"It's small enough to fit in my pack, and folded up, the mirror won't break," she said.

"How practical," Mudd said, turning his attention back to the puzzle. A memory of Hector's smiling face flashed into his mind. He pushed it aside and focused his concentration on the tangled pieces of metal.

"Stop, thief!" A cry rose from the street ahead.

Mudd looked up to see a short figure hurtling toward him. He would have thought it was a small human boy except for his long pointed ears, which gave him away as a kender—a fun-loving race of wanderers whose curiosity often got them in trouble. A torn and stained white robe fluttered around the kender as he raced down the street. His skin was stretched tight over his bones, and his cheeks were sunken with starvation.

He skidded to a stop in front of Mudd, eyes wide with fear. "Here," he said, shoving a glittering object into Mudd's hands.

As Mudd fumbled to hold it, his puzzle clattered to the ground.

"Be careful. It's priceless," the kender chirped. "Give it to the clerics."

A dozen white-robed clerics dashed up the road toward them.

The kender darted away, but Drakecutter snagged him by his long tangled hair and lifted him off the ground.

"Let me go. Let me go!" the kender shrieked.

Mudd frowned. The object the kender had been carrying rested lightly in his hands. He held it out to get a better look and gasped.

Thin silver filaments held a brilliant array of diamonds in the shape of Paladine's constellation, the Valiant Warrior. It gave Mudd the impression of staring up at the night sky into the face of the god Paladine himself.

The clerics halted in front of Mudd, breathless from their chase.

"Is this yours?" Mudd asked, handing the constellation to them.

"Yes," a tall cleric said. He opened a velvet-lined box and slid the constellation inside. Then he marched over to the squirming kender. "As soon as the guards get here, I'm going to make sure you spend plenty of time in prison thinking about your offense against Paladine."

The kender's skeletal face flushed. "E'li as my witness, I didn't mean to take it."

"Blasphemy," the cleric roared.

The kender kicked at Drakecutter, trying to free himself. In his struggling, a platinum medallion around his neck in the shape of a dragon slipped out of his robes and glimmered in the setting sun.

"I suppose you stole that as well," the cleric said. "Hand it over so I can find the rightful owner."

"No, it's mine. Elistan gave it to me." The kender stopped struggling and somehow made himself look graceful and regal while being held above the ground by his hair.

Mudd blinked. Mudd had only known one kender personally, his old friend Sindri Suncatcher, and in all the time Mudd had spent with him, the kender had never once shown fear or looked so poised. In fact, Mudd was pretty sure that kender weren't supposed to be able to feel afraid of anything.

"I don't think so," the cleric told the kender. He reached for the medallion.

"Stop in the name of Paladine," the kender cried. A bright light flashed from the medallion, long and blinding. The cleric flew backward and landed several feet away.

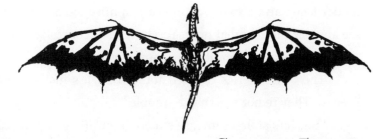

Chapter Fifteen

Mudd rubbed his eyes, trying to see again after the bright flash. The street fell silent and everyone nearby gathered in an astonished circle around them.

Drakecutter growled and dropped the kender. The skeletal figure landed on wobbly feet and wrapped his hand around the medallion. He stood for a moment with a look of bliss on his face before collapsing to the ground unconscious.

The cleric got to his feet and brushed himself off. His cheeks burned red, and he charged back toward the kender.

"Leave him alone." Hiera stepped in front of the fallen kender and drew her long knives.

"How dare you draw weapons against me?" the cleric said. "I am Bregan, a Revered Son of Paladine. Step aside, or I'll have you thrown in prison along with the kender."

Hiera set her stance and glared at him. "You profess to follow Paladine, yet you would throw this kender in prison? He's wasting away—he'd die there! Do what you think you must, but I will give my own life defending him if you try it."

Mudd's heart raced, and he grabbed Hiera's arm. "Revered Son, please forgive my sister," Mudd said, bowing. "She has a tender heart and a sword arm that is a mite too quick. I don't see any need for combat here. You have your constellation, and the kender is in no condition to cause you any trouble."

The other clerics hurried forward. "He's just a kender, Bregan. They're not worth the trouble."

"But he's stolen someone's medallion." Bregan pointed to the disk with a platinum dragon on it that still hung around the kender's neck.

The clerics all reached for their own medallions, double-checking that it wasn't theirs the kender had swiped. All were in place.

Hiera pulled away from Mudd. "If Paladine wanted you to have the kender's medallion, why did he smite you when you tried to take it? Maybe this Elistan guy did give it to him."

"Show a little respect," Bregan shouted. "Revered Son Elistan is Paladine's chosen vessel. He was one of the first to bring the knowledge of the true gods to Palanthas."

Mudd gave the cleric a humble smile. "Perhaps the matter could be settled by simply asking Revered Son Elistan about it."

"I was on my way to speak to Elistan on the kender's behalf when the little rat made off with the sacred Constellation of Paladine."

"An unfortunate turn of events," Mudd said. His mind spun. If he couldn't resolve this, Hiera would end up in prison alongside the kender.

"I have an idea," Mudd said. "We're going to be staying right over there at that inn. He and the medallion can stay with us while you return to your temple and see if there are any missing medallions."

Bregan glared at Mudd and took a firm step toward Hiera. The other clerics stopped him. "Come on, Bregan. You saw the light and felt Paladine's power. What the boy says makes sense," one of the clerics pointed out. "Let's go back to the temple and discuss this with Revered Son Elistan."

Bregan hesitated, but allowed his companions to pull him away. "All right," Bregan said, striding away down the street. "But I assure you that Elistan has never ordained a kender."

Hiera sheathed her knives and knelt beside the fallen kender. "Look at him, Mudd. He's practically starved to death."

Mudd retrieved his puzzle from the ground and slipped it in his pocket. Then he lifted the ragged kender in his arms and headed for the inn.

"Hiera, I'm going to kill you," he said through clenched teeth. "We're supposed to be saving Shemnara, not throwing our lives away on a complete stranger."

"I think Shemnara would approve," Hiera snapped.

"You are one crazy girl," Drakecutter grumbled. "Drawing weapons against a cleric of Paladine. They caught the thief red-handed, stealing that constellation thing. What was the point in defending him?"

"Shut up," Hiera said. "I happen to know a kender, and they're not really the thieves most people think they are."

Mudd carried the near-weightless kender to the door of the inn and sent Drakecutter inside to arrange them a room.

The Paladine's Prize was a two-story building made of sparkling white stone. The front doors were polished mahogany, and a dragon fountain out front sent a spray of tinkling water into the air.

Drakecutter returned and motioned Mudd and Hiera inside. They passed through a cheery common room where a dozen patrons sat chatting over an evening meal of roast beef and candied carrots. Mudd's stomach protested about leaving the rich food behind as he climbed the stairs to their chambers.

Drakecutter had procured them two adjoining rooms, one for Hiera and the other for the rest. The furnishings were simple but clean. Late evening sunlight came in through a wide window in the boys' room. Mudd laid the unconscious kender on the bed.

"He'll need a bath and some new clothes," Hiera said, propping her bow up against a sturdy table that sat next to the wall. "Better light a fire too and get some food for him. Mudd, have you ever seen anyone so thin?"

Mudd thumped his pack onto the table and took a deep breath. "No, Hiera, never. It's getting late. I'm going over to the library to see what I can find. Save some dinner for me." He strode to the door. He couldn't let this kender get in the way of finding the dragon pendant and saving Shemnara.

Drakecutter moved to follow him. Mudd waved him back. "You better stay here and make sure that kender doesn't run off.

Who knows what Revered Son Bregan will do if he comes and the kender isn't here?"

Mudd's stomach growled in protest as he hurried down the street toward the great library. He was in the inner rings of the city now and could see a tall black tower to his left that made his neck hair stand on end. That had to be the Tower of High Sorcery. Just the sight of the cursed tower made him shudder.

Across from it, a shining white marble edifice defied the tower's darkness. Mudd guessed it must be the Temple of Paladine, since the clerics had headed off in that direction.

The Great Library of Palanthas filled a whole block just ahead. A set of curved stairs led up to the main wing of the large marble building. Four pillars framed the glass-paned entryway.

Mudd started up the steps, but a man in a fancy purple doublet called him back to the street. "You won't be let in that way, boy. The main hall is closed to the public and guarded by the Aesthetics in the library that serve Astinus. That wing over there is the public section." The man pointed to a small wing off to the left.

Mudd thanked him, and the man hurried away muttering about uneducated country youth.

Mudd took a deep breath and looked at himself. He was a little on the rougher side from all his travel. He tried to brush the dust from the journey off his clothes, and when he was a little more presentable, he marched up the steps to a small wooden door in the public wing. But it was locked. His hand went to the hidden pocket in his shirt, but he stopped himself and knocked instead.

After a few moments, the door swung open to reveal a stern-faced middle-aged man in a flowing robe. "How may I help you?" The tone of his voice said he had no desire to help Mudd at all.

Mudd gave the Aesthetic a friendly smile. "I need to look something up in the library."

"Very well," the man said, but his body blocked the entrance. "You may conduct your research ten days from now when the public section reopens."

Mudd's jaw dropped. "Reopens? But—"

"Of course." The Aesthetic sniffed and smoothed his robes. "The notice of the closure has been posted for months. Spring cleaning."

"But I just got to Palanthas. I couldn't have seen the notice," Mudd argued. "And this is a matter of life and death."

"Research always is," the Aesthetic said gravely, then swung the door shut in Mudd's face.

CHAPTER SIXTEEN

Mudd stopped in the common room and helped himself to what remained of dinner. The tender roast warmed his stomach but could not ease his frustration with the Aesthetic at the library. His left hand rested against the small bundle in his shirt while he devoured the candied carrots. With the proper tools, he could gain access to anything.

His anger succumbed to new excitement. Forget the public section. If he had to unlock a door, it might as well be into the main library itself.

Chuckling, he headed up to his room.

He opened the door and found Drakecutter sitting in front of the fireplace, sharpening his dagger. Firelight glinted off the shining steel.

Mudd sucked in a sharp breath. He'd left Hiera alone with the dwarf. Set-ai's description of a draconian knife in the back rushed into Mudd's thoughts. Fearing for Hiera's safety, he drew his sword and lunged into the room toward Drakecutter.

Drakecutter jumped to his feet, ready to deflect Mudd's blow with the dagger.

"Mudd!" Hiera's startled exclamation stopped Mudd. She sat unharmed on the edge of the bed by the kender.

Mudd lowered his sword. His face grew hot with embarrassment.

Hiera and Drakecutter glared at him, waiting for some kind of an explanation.

Mudd cleared his throat and chuckled. "Sorry, I thought I saw a draconian. It must have been the shadows from the fire."

He sheathed his sword and went over to Hiera. "How is your little friend?"

"Still unconscious. I bought some clothes for him out in the market." A tiny pair of brown trousers and a forest-green shirt lay on the bed along with a heavy leather vest, a cloak, a sturdy pair of boots, and a set of small daggers.

Mudd rested a hand on the kender's bony arm. He was glad Hiera had saved him, but . . . Mudd pulled his hand back. "You thought of everything, I see." Mudd gestured toward the clothes. "Do we have any steel left?"

"Enough to pay for the inn. Don't worry, I'm not stupid. But it's cold out this time of year. He needs warm clothes." She brushed her fingers across the kender's brow.

The kender stirred, blinked, and looked up at Hiera.

"It's all right," Hiera cooed. "You're safe. I didn't let that rotten cleric throw you in prison."

The kender stiffened, and his hand fumbled for the medallion around his neck. "Y-you shouldn't speak that way about a Revered Son of E'li, even if he is a blundering human fool." The kender bit his lip and fell silent.

Hiera giggled and straightened the covers over the kender. "Who's E'li? Some god? I've never heard of him."

The kender frowned and sat up. "You've never heard of E'li, the supreme leader of all the gods of good. The creator of the high and chosen race of Silvanesti elves?"

"I think he means Paladine, Hiera," Mudd said. "I've heard that the elves call him E'li." He sank into a chair next to the table and pulled out the drawing of the stone door. Somewhere in the Great Library there had to be a reference to where it was hidden.

"Oh, Paladine. Of course I know him." Hiera patted the kender's shoulder, oblivious to the look of annoyance the kender gave her for doing it. "My name's Hiera, by the way, and this is Mudd and Drakecutter. We told Revered Son Bregan we'd look after you while he went back to the temple and got everything worked out. I'm sure Revered Son Elistan will speak up for you."

The kender slithered out of the bed and straightened his tattered robes. "I thought so once, but now I'm not sure. I have been cursed. I had hoped Elistan could reverse it, but they won't even let me talk to him. No one will listen to a kender, and why should they? Kender are no more than thieving pestilences that cause disorder wherever they go." He frowned, his little hands balled into tight fists.

Mudd laid the parchment on the table and peered at the kender. He'd never known anyone to talk about his own race that way. It set Mudd's nerves on edge.

"Hiera's told you who we are," Mudd said. "Why don't you tell us who you are and what you were doing with that constellation?"

The kender puffed out his chest and lifted his chin. "I am Iroden Jalastin Endorlian, son of Arelis Keylayess Endorlian of House Cl—" He cut off midsentence and his face turned deep red. "Just call me Iroden."

"All right, Iroden," Drakecutter growled. "Why'd you steal that constellation?"

"I didn't steal it." Iroden's voice rose to a high squeak. "I was just looking at it, and Bregan started after me. I couldn't drop it, or it would have been dashed to pieces. I couldn't let him catch me because he wouldn't listen, and he would have thrown me in prison. That's why I gave it to Mudd." Iroden shook with anger.

"Leave him alone," Hiera told Mudd and Drakecutter. "Can't you see he's been through enough already? He doesn't need you two hounding him."

Hiera scooped up the bundle of clothes and handed them to Iroden. "There's a bath for you in the other room, and here are some new clothes. When you're done, you can eat. I saved plenty of food for you."

"You want me to wear *these?*" he cried in dismay.

Hiera stepped back, looking hurt. "I used all the extra steel

I had to buy them for you. I wanted you to be warm."

Iroden dropped his gaze to the clothes and fingered the material. He opened his mouth to say something, paused, then closed it. "Thank you," he finally blurted out, then flung himself into the adjoining room and closed the door.

Drakecutter grunted and came over to the table where Mudd sat with the parchment. "Did you find anything at the library?"

Mudd grimaced. "It's closed for spring cleaning."

Hiera dropped onto the bed. "It can't be!" she cried. "Mudd, we'll have to go back tomorrow morning. If we tell them about the red dragon and Shemnara, they'll have to help us. Anyone can see how important this is."

"Of course we'll go back," Mudd said, running his fingers along the runes in the picture. The dried ink tickled his fingertips. But he intended to go back to the library far sooner than morning.

A plate of food sat on the table along with a flagon of punch. Mudd reached for it while he puzzled over the picture.

"Hands off." Hiera slapped Mudd's fingers. "That food's for Iroden. You already ate."

Mudd half smiled. This new kender often made him remember the times he'd spent with his old friend Sindri. Sindri had shared Mudd's enthusiasm for life and love of adventure. This kender—the only other kender Mudd had met—didn't seem as energetic as Sindri.

After long minutes of just staring at the picture, Mudd

leaned back and rubbed his eyes. "If we could just read these awful runes."

"What runes?" Iroden stood in the doorway, washed and dressed, running his fingers through his hopelessly tangled hair.

"Nothing." Mudd reached for the parchment to fold it and put it away, but Hiera picked it up first.

"These runes," she said, holding up the picture. "We've got to find this door, but we don't know what this says."

Iroden took the parchment from Hiera and studied it for a moment. "These are Draconic runes. It's seldom that any race other than the dragons get a chance to see them. Certainly the dragons don't go around sharing them with humans and dwarves. How did you come by this?"

Drakecutter growled and snatched the drawing from Iroden. "What do you know of dragons, kender? This is none of your affair. We saved your miserable life. That doesn't give you the right to insult us."

Mudd stood and held out his hand to Drakecutter. "Give me the picture," he said, trying not to sound testy. He trusted it in Drakecutter's hands even less than Iroden's.

Drakecutter passed it to Mudd and stomped back over to sit by the fire. Mudd folded the parchment and stuffed it in his pocket.

"Ignore Drakecutter," Hiera said. "His father has been badly injured and might die soon if we don't find that door quickly. And the holy woman from my village has been taken by a red dragon. This door is the only chance we have of finding—"

"Hiera!" Mudd shouted before she could tell Iroden about the dragon pendant. It was bad enough they had to bring Drakecutter along.

Hiera put her hands on her hips, but Iroden spoke before she could start an argument with Mudd.

"I get the idea. Something valuable lies behind the door. I'm not going to try to steal it. I promise you. Since you have helped me, I will tell you what the runes say."

Mudd listened begrudgingly. Kender tended to travel widely. If somewhere Iroden had learned to read Draconic runes, so much the better.

"You may be disappointed, though. They don't give direction to the door's location." Iroden raised his arm in a regal gesture that might have looked magnificent if made by an elf, but seemed laughable for a kender. "The runes inscribed above the doorway say 'Only the True Heart May Pass.'"

CHAPTER SEVENTEEN

Mudd paced the room, fingering his lock picks. No closed library or cryptic runes would stop him from getting the pendant and saving Shemnara. It couldn't.

Hiera had wilted onto a chair upon hearing Iroden's translation of the runes, but now she was up and busy again, ushering Iroden over to the table and offered him the delicious-smelling roast she'd saved. Iroden hesitated before climbing onto the chair.

"Why are you helping me?" he asked.

"Why shouldn't we help you?" Hiera said, wrapping her arms around him, giving a tight squeeze, and depositing him on the chair. "Now eat up, but don't make yourself sick. You'll get breakfast tomorrow too, so don't worry."

A look of annoyance slipped across Iroden's face, but he smiled again before Hiera could see it. "Thank you, Hiera," he said, giving Mudd a questioning look as if to ask if she were always like this.

Mudd rolled his eyes and nodded. He slumped onto the

bed, pulled out the puzzle he'd purchased, and fiddled with the cool metal strands.

Iroden took slow deliberate bites, eating with such fastidiousness that Mudd felt like rushing to the table and shoving the food down for him. What kender ate so slowly? Kender were known for their voracious appetites. What a strange kender this one was.

Hiera sat beside Iroden and filled the room with a steady chatter about their kender friend Sindri and other mundane topics until she worked her way around to the red dragon's attack on Potter's Mill. Mudd interrupted the conversation there and suggested they all get some sleep.

"Fine," Hiera said, jumping up. "But you're going to have to tell him about the silver dragon sooner or later."

Mudd glared at her.

Iroden dabbed his mouth with a napkin and climbed down from the chair. "Mudd has no reason to trust me with delicate information. Tomorrow you will hear back from the temple that I have stolen nothing, and I will be gone. But you three must find a way to save your loved ones. I will ask E'li's blessing to be upon you." He sank to his knees beside the bed and fingered his medallion while muttering a soft prayer.

Mudd stifled a laugh, realizing finally why Iroden had been dismayed at the clothes Hiera had bought him.

"What?" Hiera whispered.

Mudd drew her into the other room before bursting out into full laughter. "Iroden must think he's a cleric of Paladine.

He'd have been happier if you'd gotten him a white robe."

"What's so funny about that?" Hiera put her hands on her hips and glared at Mudd. "Perhaps he is."

Mudd pulled himself together. "I've never heard of a kender cleric. Have you? Not that I mind. He can be a cleric if he wants. Sorry I laughed."

"Good night, Mudd," Hiera said firmly, pushing him back into his own room. Mudd gave her a hug and retreated, still chuckling under his breath.

Iroden finished his prayer and stood, hovering beside the bed. There was only one bed, and three people to share it.

"Go ahead and have it," Mudd said. "I'm just as happy on the floor." He got out his bedroll and spread it in front of the door.

Iroden slipped under the covers, but his eyes remained open.

Grumbling, Drakecutter lay down in front of the fire and fell asleep. Soon, his snores resonated through the room.

Mudd tossed and turned on his bedroll, fingering his lock picks, waiting for Iroden to sleep. Finally he gave up, threw the blanket off and stood.

"I'm going downstairs for a bit," he whispered. "Keep your eye on Drakecutter while I'm gone."

Iroden blinked in surprise. "Why? Don't you trust him?"

"Yes, I trust *Drakecutter*." Mudd stared at the sleeping dwarf for a moment. "I just don't know if he is Drakecutter. The red dragon is working with a human . . . or a sivak draconian. You know, a shapechanger. Drakecutter was separated from us for a while." Mudd shrugged. "It makes me nervous."

Iroden shuddered. "Draconians. Foul beasts. Drakecutter seems genuine dwarf to me, but I'll be cautious just the same."

Mudd slipped out the door, grinning. "Cautious" could hardly be used to describe any kender.

Downstairs, a fire still burned in the large stone fireplace in the common room. One of the other guests sat huddled beside it with the hood of his cloak drawn down over his face. The rows of long tables were dark and empty.

Mudd strode through the room and let himself outside. Night had descended over Palanthas. The streets were silent except for the rustle of wind in the leaves. The shops and merchant stalls had closed, and stars glittered overhead.

Mudd kept in the shadow of the trees that lined the road as he made his way back to the library. City smells still lingered on the air—the scent of horses and humans, the faint odor of cherry pie and roast chicken.

A door slammed somewhere far off. Mudd jumped. This wasn't like sneaking around Potter's Mill. Here, city guards patrolled the streets, and he probably wasn't the only person outside at this hour. Mudd felt open and exposed as he slipped through the shadows from tree to tree. The soft sound of a footfall behind him made him freeze.

He peered into the darkness, and saw nothing but the shadow of leaves cast on the ground by the starlight. He shrugged and continued on to his destination, still wary of what city eyes might think a boy would be doing in the street this late.

It wasn't far before the massive library loomed out of the darkness. Mudd left the road and darted into the gardens behind the building, where the trees were tall and ancient. He pressed up against a wide trunk and patted the gnarly bark. If the tree could talk, it could probably tell the history of Krynn better than any musty old scribe writing away in a library.

Moving from tree to tree, Mudd inched up to the building, looking for a back door. There it was, a shadowy rectangle against the marble walls.

Sliding his lock picks out, Mudd dashed to the door and got to work. His heart pounded while his deft fingers inserted two thin metal rods into the lock. Solamnic locks were all too easy, but this one refused to budge. Sweat broke out on his forehead as he remembered Drakecutter saying Palanthas had been built by dwarves. Dwarven locks were another matter.

Mudd huddled against the door and ran his fingers through his small bundle of tools. Choosing another set, he slid them into the lock. His mouth grew dry.

Out of the corner of his eye he saw a shadow move in the trees. He whirled around, clutching the lock picks like tiny daggers.

The trees swayed in the wind. An owl hooted and then fell silent. Nothing moved.

Mudd took a deep breath and went back to the lock. At last it clicked open. Mudd eased through the door and found himself in a dark room. The caustic scent of lime hung heavy on the air, making his eyes water.

He closed the door behind him and set about lighting a small lantern, wishing he had one of Hector's quicklamps that could be lit with the twist of a knob. Sneaking about had been so much easier with the inventions of his gnome friend.

When the wavering flame finally lit, Mudd closed the lantern's shutter halfway and held it up. His lantern illuminated only a few feet at a time, but as Mudd continued through the room he saw that large vats with animal pelts soaking in lime filled the room. At the far end, a row of skins with the hair scraped off had been stretched on frames to dry.

So that's how they make parchment, Mudd thought as he wove his way through the vats. He'd have loved to be there during the day to watch the Aesthetics work. "Not that they'd let me in," he muttered under his breath.

Mudd stepped from that room into a long hall. Snores from behind a row of doors told him those were the Aesthetics' quarters. He hurried past as quiet as he could on tiptoe.

Near the end of the hall, a set of ornately carved double doors caught his attention. These, too, were locked, but he got through them faster now that he had figured out the backdoor lock.

Excitement rushed through him. Beyond the doors lay the forbidden library—forbidden to everyone but him.

The doors swung open.

He'd gotten in. Now he need only glance through the books until he found mention of the dragon pendant.

Mudd held up his lantern and in the circle of light it cast

around him, he saw a tall bookshelf ornamented in the same style as the doors. He ran his fingers along the smooth wood, feeling the leaves and flowers and Solamnic symbols that had been carved into it. The room smelled like polished wood and ancient leather.

Grinning, Mudd started along the shelf, examining each precious book. The first was a manual about proper fishing methods in Newsea. Another gave detailed descriptions of the anatomy of various frogs.

It took him half an hour to go through a dozen books, but he didn't find anything useful. No problem, there were still at least fifty more books. He took a couple of steps along the bookshelf, just reading the titles. Nothing looked promising. He was surprised to see that the bookshelf continued farther into the darkness.

"Let's just see how many chances I have to find this," he whispered to himself. He took a few more steps. The bookshelf kept going.

More steps only showed more of the same bookshelf. He walked faster, forcing his eyes to scan the titles of books he passed. Still the ornate bookshelf continued on into the darkness.

He broke into a run, disbelief welling up in him. The books couldn't go on forever. But they seemed to. He was panting hard by the time he reached the end of the bookshelf. He lifted his lantern and saw more bookshelves on either side of the first.

"How many are there?" he said. He started running along the ends of the bookshelves. He counted: one, two, three, four . . . twenty-five . . . eighty-nine . . . one hundred. He reached the library wall and found it lined with canisters filled with scrolls.

He slumped against the last bookshelf and groaned. He'd never imagined so many books. He knew it was called the Great Library, but he figured it might have a couple hundred or so books. That would be a lot more than Mayor Shelton had in his library. Mudd could search through these books until he died of old age before he found any reference to the dragon pendant.

This far back in the library, the musty scent of the parchment and leather bindings hung heavier in the air as if these books and scrolls were older than those by the door.

Mudd's heart raced. Now what? Shemnara's life depended on him finding the dragon pendant.

Swallowing the bitter taste in his mouth, he set the lantern on the floor and pulled a heavy book from the shelf. The cover was thick and rough, and the pages crackled as he opened them. He couldn't read the flowing script inside. He'd never even seen the language before.

Defeated, he put the book on the shelf and shuffled back the way he'd come. Before he got very far, he heard voices in the hall.

"There's someone in the library. I heard scuffling," a man said. Probably an Aesthetic.

"Rats again, do you think?" a woman answered.

"I haven't seen any in the traps for a long time," said the man.

"Look, the doors are open." The woman's voice went from curious to alarmed.

Mudd blew out the lantern and flattened himself against a bookshelf.

Two Aesthetics hurried in, both carrying lamps that sent slivers of light between the long shelves and deepened the shadows beyond them.

CHAPTER EIGHTEEN

Mudd pressed himself against the back of the tall bookshelf and watched the lantern light flit between the books.

The man and woman split up, the woman walking along the front of the room checking each aisle, while the man rushed to the back.

Mudd's heart beat in time with the man's heavy footsteps. The woman's lighter steps scraped against the marble floor to Mudd's other side. It wouldn't be long before they came even with the aisle where he hid and saw him. They had him trapped between them with nowhere to run.

Mudd crouched down and silently pulled a set of heavy books off the bottom shelf. He stacked them on the edge of the shelf above, then waited.

Thump thump. The man's lantern lit up the back wall and cast wavering shadows on the scrolls. *Scrape.* The woman neared from the front of the room. A few more steps and they'd both reach the aisle where Mudd crouched.

Mudd licked his lips. Light filled the aisle just before his.

Then it dimmed as the two Aesthetics took the step past the ends of the bookshelf.

In that heartbeat, Mudd dived through the small hole he'd made at the bottom of the shelf and rolled into the aisle they'd already passed.

He leaped to his feet and ran for the door, grateful for the times he'd spent creeping about Potter's Mill, where he learned to run quickly and quietly. He kept to the dark shadows cast by the lanterns on the other side of the bookshelf.

Reaching the door, he swung out into the hall and rushed back toward the room with the vats.

Once inside, he closed the door and took a deep breath. The smell of the lime in the air burned his lungs. He coughed, and the ragged sound echoed through the silent building.

He pressed his hand over his mouth and rushed out of the library, taking only a moment to relock the door and shut it behind him.

The ancient trees stood sentinel outside. He slid behind a thick trunk, gasping for breath. The scent of rain hung on the air, and clouds that had not been there before billowed in the sky above him.

Dread filled him. He'd failed to find anything that would lead him to the door. He imagined Shemnara injured and hurting, imprisoned by the hungry red dragon. How long would she last against such a powerful dragon? How would he ever figure this out in time?

Mudd made his way back up the street. The bitter taste

of lime stayed with him.

A drop of water hit his nose, followed by several more. With a clap of thunder the clouds opened up and poured sheets of rain down on him. He ran for the inn.

Footsteps echoed behind him. He glanced over his shoulder, but could see nothing through the blinding rain. The hairs on the back of his neck prickled, and he ran faster.

Hiera met him at the inn's door. "Where have you been?" she demanded.

Mudd slid inside and closed the door, wiping the water out of his eyes. "I went to the library to see if I could find what we needed." His teeth chattered from the cold and wet.

"You snuck in there?" Hiera's shrill voice echoed through the common room.

"Shhh," Mudd pressed his hand over her mouth and pulled her upstairs. They reached her room before he released her.

"You should have told me," Hiera said. "I've been worried sick."

"You should be asleep," Mudd said.

"It was my half of the night to keep an eye on Drakecutter. Have you forgotten about that little problem?" Hiera shoved a towel into Mudd's hands.

"No, I haven't," Mudd said, rubbing the towel over his dripping hair and clothes. "That's why you had your own room with a lock on the door." He turned to go into his room, but Hiera stopped him with a hand on his arm.

"Did you find anything?" she asked.

That was the question Mudd was dreading. He'd hoped to slip back in without anyone noticing, so he'd never have to admit his defeat at the library.

"No. I didn't learn what we needed," Mudd said. "The library is too big. We could read through books for a hundred years and never find it. I think Drakecutter had the right idea. We have to hunt the red dragon and rescue Shemnara ourselves."

Hiera didn't say anything for a moment. Water dripped from Mudd's clothes and formed a puddle at his feet despite his best efforts with the flimsy towel.

Hiera frowned. "The Aesthetics know the library well. They could guide us to a likely section of books that would only take us a short time to find mention of the pendant."

"Except the Aesthetics won't let us in, remember?" Mudd said.

"We'll just have to try again in the morning. I'm sure the Aesthetics can be reasoned with. A little bit of cleaning shouldn't be an excuse to close the whole library, especially for something as important as this." Hiera patted his back and let him go.

Mudd stalked into his own room and shut the door.

Sunlight shining through the window woke Mudd the next morning. Iroden was already up, kneeling in the shaft of light with his head bowed and the medallion clutched in his little hands. He wore the new clothing Hiera had gotten him, but with an air of discomfort Mudd couldn't miss.

Mudd slipped into his clothes, which he'd laid out by the fire to dry before going to sleep. Then he shook Drakecutter awake. Drakecutter snorted and slapped Mudd away. Hiera stepped into the room already dressed, holding her red comb in her hand.

Iroden stood and gave her a graceful bow that would have looked regal if he were a bit taller and dressed in robes.

"You look well," Hiera said. "If we get a few more meals into you, you'll be as good as ever. Here." She held out her comb to Iroden.

Iroden touched his tangled mop of hair and flushed with embarrassment.

Mudd grinned, gave Drakecutter one more nudge, then headed downstairs to see about breakfast. The others came down just after Mudd had finished his second helping of sausage and eggs, claiming seats at the long table beside him.

The room bustled with activity. The innkeeper's pretty daughters carried out plates of food and saw to the guests' needs. A blazing fire crackled in the fireplace. The chatter of conversation filled the room.

At one table, three fair-skinned Silvanesti elves whispered to each other, ignoring everyone else in the room. Their faces were narrow, almost delicate, and long pointed ears peeked out from beneath their golden hair. Not far from them, a table full of visiting merchants argued about acceptable pricing of their wares and preferred market locations.

The lone man Mudd had seen by the fire the night before

sat at a table as close to the warmth as he could get. From deep beneath his hood, his eyes darted about the room. His hand rested on one of his two sword hilts.

As Mudd mopped up more eggs with a bit of toast, the man pulled opened a scroll case and drew forth a single sheet of parchment. This he held and studied with great care. Mudd put a guilty hand to his pocket where he'd carelessly folded and shoved Shemnara's drawing of the door.

The innkeeper stepped into the common room holding a sealed letter. "Iroden Jalastin Endorlian," he called out, heading for the elves.

The elves looked up in surprise, and each shook his head.

Iroden jumped to his feet and strode across the room, a tiny skeletal figure lost in the press of larger beings.

"Endorlian," the innkeeper called out again. "Is there anyone here by the name of Iroden Endorlian?"

"Here!" Iroden's shrill voice cut through the chatter in the room. He reached up to take the letter. "I'm Iroden. May I have that please?"

The innkeeper frowned at Iroden and kept hold of the letter. "Don't be ridiculous. Iroden is a Silvanesti name, and this was just brought by an acolyte from the Temple of Paladine. It's sealed by Revered Son Elistan himself."

"Yes, I've been expecting it," Iroden said, drawing himself up to his full diminutive height.

Mudd jumped to his feet and crossed the room. "The

kender is Iroden," Mudd told the innkeeper. "And I was with him yesterday when the clerics said they would take his petition to Elistan. The letter is for him."

The innkeeper let out an exasperated breath and handed the letter to Iroden.

"Wait!" One of the elves stepped forward, his brow raised. "This kender is not Iroden. He should be thrown in prison for such an outrageous lie. Arelis Keylayess Endorlian is a great leader of Silvanesti House Cleric. Iroden is his son."

Iroden's face turned scarlet and his hand shook on the letter. He looked like he might say something, but instead he darted away through the common room and back up the stairs.

Mudd shrugged. "He's a bit addled. Thinks he's a cleric of Paladine, told the priests his name is Iroden. I'm sure Revered Son Elistan knows better and has taken that into account in his letter."

The elf returned to his table, giving Mudd a skeptical look. Mudd started after Iroden and found Hiera and Drakecutter right beside him.

"Poor Iroden," Hiera said. "We'd better go make sure he's all right."

Mudd led the way upstairs to their room. They found Iroden sitting at the table with the open letter crumpled in his hand. Moisture glinted at the edges of his eyes.

Hiera rushed over to him. "What does it say, Iroden? What's wrong?"

Iroden shook his head, unable to speak.

Mudd pried the crumpled letter from his fingers, smoothed it and read aloud:

> *Dear Iroden,*
>
> *I'm alarmed to hear of your present circumstances and have spent all night in prayer to Paladine on your behalf. If you return to the temple, I'll see that you are welcomed as you deserve. However, my prayers have led me to believe that the answer to your distress cannot be found here. Paladine has consecrated you in service to others who are in need of your skills. Paladine's blessing and my own go with you on whatever road you are called to follow.*
>
> *Revered Son Elistan*

"What present circumstances?" Hiera whispered.

Iroden stood, shaking. "I'm cursed. Thrust down into this vile little body. Expelled from Silvanesti society. Misused, misbelieved, mishandled. Forced to beg for scraps of food because I'm not truly a lying little thief of a kender. I'm a Silvanesti elf of House Cleric! My great skills in history, writing, translation, and healing go unused and unwanted because no one believes kender are worth anything at all. Revered Son Elistan was my last hope. Now I have nothing."

Hiera knelt and wrapped her arms around Iroden. "You have us, and I don't believe kender really set out to lie or steal. Things just happen."

Iroden struggled out of her grasp. "You don't even believe I really am Iroden Endorlian. Just because I don't look like an elf, you think I can't possibly be one."

Mudd took a deep breath. "Perhaps you'd like to tell us how you became a kender."

CHAPTER NINETEEN

"How I became a kender is none of your business," Iroden snapped. He took the letter from Mudd and strode to the door.

Frowning, Mudd shoved his hand in his pocket and fingered the puzzle. He hadn't meant to drive Iroden away. He just wanted to learn more about him.

Iroden paused before leaving the room. "Thank you," he said, his voice softening. "For the clothing, the food, and a good night's sleep in a real bed. It's been a long time since I've had those things. Good luck on your quest."

"Wait." Something inside screamed for Mudd to be quiet and let Iroden leave, but he ignored it. Instead he thought of the axe wound Set-ai had once gotten that had festered and eventually caused Set-ai to lose that arm. "Revered Son Elistan said you were to help others who are in need of your skills."

If they'd had a cleric with them, Set-Ai's wound could have been healed, and Set-ai wouldn't have lost his arm. "If you truly are a cleric, we could use your help," Mudd said.

Hiera squealed and clapped her hands. "Oh I knew you'd

come around, Mudd. Of course Iroden has to stay with us. Revered Son Elistan said he should help someone. You will help us, won't you, Iroden?"

Iroden clenched his fists and stared at Mudd, Hiera, and Drakecutter for a long moment. Finally he nodded. "It seems I have nowhere else to go for now. I might as well help you find this door and whatever lies behind it."

"Great," Mudd said. "I guess we go back to the library." He led the others downstairs.

They crossed the crowded common room and had almost reached the door when Mudd heard a snatch of conversation that made him stop.

The hooded man was paying the innkeeper for the night's lodging. "Hurry," the man said. "I've got an appointment with Bertrem at the library in a few minutes."

The innkeeper took his steel and handed back his change in coppers. "Kirak, do you think he's found what you're looking for this time? I will sorely miss your patronage if he has."

"Kirak?" Hiera's high-pitched voice cut through the noise in the room.

Kirak started and turned toward them, pushing back his hood. Mudd sucked in a sharp breath. The long dark hair and silver eyes were unmistakable. He was the boy for whom Shemnara had received the silver dragon vision.

Hiera rushed over and gave him a tight hug. Mudd shook his head at his sister's impulsive affection. He doubted she would ever change.

Kirak's eyes widened at Hiera's hug. "Do I know you?"

Mudd pulled Hiera away. "You may not remember us. I'm Mudd and this is Hiera. We're from Potter's Mill, where you visited the seer Shemnara a few years back." Though Mudd had grown since then, Kirak still towered over him.

Kirak frowned, and his fingers wrapped around the scroll case he'd had out earlier. "I remember Shemnara, but not either of you."

Drakecutter stepped up beside Mudd and Hiera. "And I suppose you don't remember me either, though you stayed at my father's house for weeks while you poked about in the mountains above our village."

Kirak gave Drakecutter a grim smile. "I could never forget your father's hospitality while I pursued my quest, nor you, *Greenthumb*."

At the mention of his first name, Drakecutter growled and stepped toward Kirak. Mudd grabbed his shoulder. A jolt went through Mudd as he realized Kirak's quest was the same as his own. Shemnara had sent Kirak after the dragon pendant first.

"Kirak," Hiera chirped. "Did you find it? Did you find the pendant? Because Shemnara's in trouble and we really need it."

Mudd winced. Trust Hiera to blurt things out.

Though the troublesome elves were gone, Iroden stayed behind Mudd and Drakecutter, unnoticed. A few people nearby had paused in their breakfasting to stare at the impromptu reunion.

Kirak drew his cloak over the scroll case and dropped his

hand to his sword. "What has happened to Shemnara?"

Aware of the many eyes in the room fixed on them after Hiera's outburst, Mudd motioned to the front door. "Perhaps we should discuss this outside."

"Yes." Kirak strode out of the inn. "And I'm late, so we'll have to talk while I head for the library." He marched down the bustling street.

Mudd hurried to keep stride with the larger boy. "Shemnara has been taken by a red dragon. She left a message that I should find the silver dragon to save her."

"So you want the pendant?" Kirak asked through gritted teeth.

Mudd nodded. He hoped Kirak would be willing to help.

"We thought to find some information about it at the library," Hiera said, oblivious to Kirak's resentment. "But the library is closed for cleaning. If you have an appointment, though, maybe you could convince them to let us in."

Drakecutter cleared his throat. "Unless you've already found the pendant, in which case you might consider letting us use it, perhaps?"

Kirak stopped, both fists on his sword hilts now, his face tense, his eyes glazed, as if fighting some inner battle. It lasted only a moment, then he dropped his gaze to stare at his boots.

"If I had the pendant, I would let you use it to save Shemnara. Unfortunately, I have not yet located it." Kirak started walking again. "Bertrem, a high senior Aesthetic, has been researching it for me. I'm going right now to see if he has found anything."

"But you'll let us come, won't you?" Hiera asked. "You will help us?"

"Yes, I'll help you." His face hardened, and a look of grim determination came into his eyes. Mudd could tell Kirak didn't want them along, but he couldn't let that stop them.

Kirak climbed the steps to the library's public wing and tried the door. To Mudd's surprise it was unlocked, and they stepped into a tall antechamber filled with sunlight.

The choking smell of wood polish hung heavy on the air. The ornate Solamnic carvings Mudd had seen on the doors and bookshelves the night before continued in the chamber's marble walls. The sounds of cleaning and the scrape of rearranging furniture came through an arched doorway.

Kirak stepped beneath the arch and called out.

A young boy, wearing an ink-stained brown apron over flowing robes, raced up and slid to a stop in front of Kirak. He held a cake of polish in one hand and a rag in the other.

"I have an appointment to see Bertrem," Kirak said.

The boy's eyes widened and he dropped the polish.

Kirak's hand shot out and caught it before it hit the floor. "Will you tell him that Kirak is here?"

"W-what? Me, go to Bertrem's office?" The boy glanced back the way he'd come. "Master Azeden," he cried.

An older Aesthetic strode into the antechamber and sent the boy scurrying back to his work. "Ah, Kirak," he said. "We've been expecting you. Unfortunately a personage of great importance arrived last night, and Bertrem is occupied at the moment. However, I have been working with him on your project and would be happy to help you."

He motioned Kirak through the arch, but held up his hand when Mudd and the others tried to follow. "I'm sorry. The library is closed today."

"It's all right. They're with me," Kirak said.

"The kender too?" Azeden asked with a grimace.

Kirak whirled around to stare at Iroden. "Mudd, is that the kender from the inn?"

"Iroden can read the runes on Shemnara's picture." Mudd rested a hand on Iroden's bony shoulder. "He's offered to help us find the door."

"Ha," the Aesthetic said. "He *says* he can read the runes. Not even I can. Only a fool would believe that from a kender."

"Perhaps he should wait outside, Mudd," Kirak said. "We don't want to have anything go missing from the library."

Hiera spluttered in outrage and reached for her long knives. To Mudd's surprise, Iroden grabbed her hand before she could draw. "Books are valuable, Hiera. You can't begin to understand the hours it takes penning each page."

He looked up at Azeden. "I can assure you I would never harm anything in this library. But since I know you won't believe me, I'll just wait outside."

"No," Hiera said.

"Iroden stays with us," Mudd agreed. "If we encounter more text like that in the drawing, we'll need him to read it. I promise I'll make sure he doesn't get into any trouble."

Azeden shook his head in exasperation. "If you hadn't donated so much steel to the library, Kirak, I would never allow this. But I suppose I have no choice. Come with me. Bertrem has selected a number of books which may or may not be of some help."

Azeden led them into a large hall where young Aesthetics scurried about, moving tables, scrubbing the floor, washing windows, and polishing lecterns that had thick books chained to them.

Mudd slipped on the soapy floor and would have fallen if Drakecutter hadn't caught him from behind. "Watch your step," the dwarf muttered.

They left the public section behind and came into a smaller room with a heavy bookshelf against one wall and a couple of tables in the middle. Two Aesthetics, an older man and a woman, stood beside several stacks of books on one of the tables.

"Oh," Azeden said. "Master Bertrem. Mistress Nitere." He bowed so deeply to the woman that his nose seemed to touch his knees. "I didn't realize you were here."

"Quite all right, Azeden," Bertrem said. He left the woman's side and drew Azeden to the door. "Nitere has decided to meet with Kirak."

Azeden stared at Kirak in startled amazement as Bertrem ushered him out of the room.

CHAPTER TWENTY

irak stared at the female Aesthetic in wonder, and a cold shiver went up his spine. Air from an open window rustled her flowing white robe, filling the room with the scent of a morning after rain. Her wavy silver hair gleamed in the sunlight. Radiance glowed from her flawless face. She was the most beautiful woman Kirak had ever seen.

From the looks on the others' faces, Kirak guessed they felt the same way.

"Welcome," Nitere said. Her voice brought to mind the rush of wind through vast blue skies. "Master Bertrem tells me you are looking for something. Perhaps I can help. You have a picture, I believe."

Nitere smiled and held out her left hand. A bandage wrapped her right arm, and a sling held it in place by her side.

Kirak drew out his scroll case and eased the parchment with Shemnara's drawing from inside. Before he could get it unrolled, Mudd thrust a folded and battered parchment into her hand. Kirak gritted his teeth to suppress his annoyance.

Nitere unfolded it and laid it on the table, then took Kirak's picture. She set it down beside the first. "You're all looking for this same thing, I take it?"

A stab of guilt went through Kirak. Yes, because of him, they were.

Nitere looked at Mudd for a moment then shifted her gaze to Hiera and Drakecutter. When her gaze fell on Iroden, her lips curled in amusement. Last of all she rested her mercury-colored eyes on Kirak.

He winced as those eyes bore deep into his soul. They sifted through his mind, flowing like quicksilver to the dark places he shunned.

He stumbled back and tried to break eye contact, but Nitere wrapped a gentle hand around his arm. Her gaze pierced all the way to the darkest place of all, his earliest memory, a time of terror and pain when he'd fought for his life against the demon that would have destroyed him.

Kirak could not stop the strangled cry of pain that burst from his lips.

Nitere released him and looked away. "I cannot help you," she whispered, then turned and fled from the room. As she passed the bookshelf beside the door, her robe brushed a stack of books, knocking one of them to the floor with a loud thump.

Kirak shuddered. Sweat covered him, and his hands shook.

Frowning, Mudd walked over and picked up the book the Aesthetic had knocked to the floor. The ragged cover was rough against his fingers, and it smelled like dirt and sweat. A dark stain that looked suspiciously like blood marred the back

"That was odd," Drakecutter said, staring after the fleeing Aesthetic.

"She probably got a whiff of your bad breath." Hiera shoved the dwarf away from her.

"What? I don't have bad breath," Drakecutter grumbled.

"Stop it," Mudd said. "We have better things to do than argue. Look at all these books. It could take us days to find what we need."

Beneath his stern words, Mudd's heart raced with excitement. This smaller number of books he could handle, compared to the endless volumes he'd encountered in the main library.

He took the odd book to a table and sat down. The cover was made from plain brown fabric. The title had been penned on the front in black ink: *Fighting on the Wrong Side.*

Mudd opened the book. The front page said it was an account of one Captain Haman, leader of a band of mercenaries who had fought under the Dragon Highlords during the War of the Lance.

Reading on, Mudd learned that the book was Haman's journal, giving an account of his part in the war. Mudd didn't think it was what they were looking for, but his curiosity kept him reading.

With the arrival of the silver dragons in Palanthas and the forging of the dragonlances, Haman and his cohorts were driven back with the rest of the dragonarmies.

Haman could tell he'd joined forces with the wrong side. He and his men deserted from the dragonarmies and holed up in a cave in the Vingaard Mountains. A rough sketch in the book showed it was located in the craggy cliffs northeast of the High Clerist's Tower.

Hiera carried an armload of books to the table and thumped them down in front of her. "*Silver Mines of Solamnia.* Probably not. *The Forging of Silver.* Maybe. *Magic Artifacts of Krynn.* Hmm, this could take a while."

Iroden walked along the heavy bookshelf, glancing over the books that lined it.

Drakecutter thumped into a chair and put his feet up on the table. He pulled out his dagger.

Mudd flinched and reached for his sword.

Paying no attention to Mudd, Drakecutter used the tip of his knife to clean his fingernails.

"Are you going to help us?" Hiera asked Drakecutter.

Drakecutter mumbled something under his breath.

"What?" Hiera said.

"I said I can't read! Blast it, girl!" Drakecutter roared.

Iroden shot him a look of disdain.

Kirak lowered the book he'd been flipping through. "A little quieter, please," he said, "or they may throw us out."

"That's all right," Hiera said, patting Drakecutter's arm. "You can still look through the books for a picture of the doorway we need to find."

"Sure. Fine," Drakecutter said. He grabbed the book Mudd had been reading and fanned the pages in front of his face.

"There." He slammed the book down, pressing the pages open to a hastily scrawled drawing of a doorway with runes arching over the top.

"That's it. You found it!" Hiera squealed.

Mudd jerked the book back from Drakecutter. "I found it. I had this book first." He turned the page and read through the passages next to the picture. After all the trouble to get into the library it seemed unbelievable that they would find reference to the stone doorway so quickly. But then, Bertrem had been researching it for quite some time.

"The book says this mercenary, Haman, was holed up in a cave," Mudd explained. "One day he and his buddies decided to explore the far reaches. Something bad happened. It doesn't say what. Everyone but Haman died. He starts raving here about the locked door shown in the picture. It seems he searched the cave for the key until he ran out of food.

"He came to Palanthas to restock and go back, but he never made it out of the city. A note on the last page says his body was found. He was stabbed to death in an alley. Since there was no record of next of kin, this book was sent to the library."

Iroden pushed his way to the table and ran his finger

along the runes scribbled on the picture. "The man has terrible handwriting, but the runes are the same. *'Only the True Heart May Pass.'* I wonder what it means."

Mudd figured it might mean that draconians pretending to be dwarves were out of luck.

"I think I know," Hiera said. "Mudd, didn't Shemnara's vision say something about three tests?"

"Yes." Kirak walked to the table, moving sluggishly as if reluctant to include himself in the conversation. "She said the pendant is guarded by a test of courage, a test of love, and a test of truth."

"Right," Hiera said. "Courage, love, and truth, three things a mercenary like Haman would know nothing about."

Mudd nodded. Hiera was right. The tests were likely to weed out any riffraff. He hoped it wouldn't weed him and the others out as well.

"What does a silver dragon care about courage, love, and truth?" Drakecutter asked, stamping his foot.

Hiera glared at him. "The dragon probably wants to make sure whoever it grants a wish to is worthy of its help."

"So let me get this straight." Iroden looked up at Mudd. "We're going to find this pendant and call on the silver dragon to save Shemnara and Drakecutter's father?"

"Right," Mudd said.

"Great, but where is this cave?" Kirak interrupted. "Does the book say?" Kirak's hands rested on his sword hilts like they had when he had come to see Shemnara.

"Yes." Mudd flipped to the map and held it up for all to see. A look of despair came into Kirak's eyes, and he turned away.

Mudd lowered the book, fingering the rough brown binding. "Aren't you happy, Kirak? You've been looking for so long."

Outside the open window the wind whipped up. A cloud formed in front of the sun, casting a dark shadow on Kirak's face.

"Probably doesn't want to share the find with us," Drakecutter suggested, crossing his arms.

"But Kirak, this will be better." Hiera touched Kirak's tense arm. "Those tests could be dangerous. You don't want to face them alone, do you?"

Kirak stared at his boots for a moment. "No, I don't want to go alone," he said through gritted teeth.

"Perfect," Hiera clapped her hands in delight. "Let's go."

"Just a moment," Iroden said. "The Aesthetics won't let us take the book. We'll need to make a copy of that map. If you'll allow me." He motioned to an inkwell and stack of parchment on one of the tables.

Mudd gave him the book.

Iroden carried it over to the table, scrambled up onto the chair, and set to work. His hand moved surely and quickly as he transcribed useful passages. His ornate handwriting was flawless. Mudd watched in amazement, wondering if the kender's story could somehow be true. Iroden drew the map exactly as it appeared on the page so that Mudd couldn't tell one picture from the other.

Iroden finished the likeness and handed it over to Mudd. "Since the Aesthetic has gone, I suppose we should show ourselves out." He hopped down from the chair and headed for the door.

Mudd followed, already making plans in his mind. They needed to get their things from the inn and purchase supplies for their journey. If they hurried, they might make it out of the city before lunchtime.

CHAPTER TWENTY-ONE

Mudd's hopes for a quick exit from Palanthas were dashed when he found a pair of knights waiting for them in the common room at the inn. They greeted Mudd and Hiera and motioned for them to join their table.

"Why thank you," Hiera said, sliding into a chair.

Mudd thumped down at the table. "How can we be of service?" He strained to keep his voice polite and to sit still. He itched to be on his way after the pendant. But the older of the knights had the insignia of the rose on his armor, a rank Mudd knew he had better respect.

"My name is Sir Ollen," the knight said. "And this is my squire, Cenay. I understand you have had problems with a red dragon."

"Oh yes," Hiera said. "It was horrible." Her face twisted in dramatized fright. "The dragon came right out of the sky, tearing up the houses and burning everything. I do hope you can find and kill it."

Mudd dug his thumbnail into the edge of the wooden

table and let her talk. He doubted the knights could find the red dragon and destroy her in time to save Shemnara.

The knight peppered Hiera with questions. Which way did the dragon come from? Which way did it go when it flew away? What time of day was it? Which buildings did it burn? How many people were killed?

Hiera flew into animated detail, using her hands to describe the whole terrible event. Mudd fidgeted while the time slipped away. He pulled out his puzzle and worked at it under the table where the knights couldn't see it. He wiggled it this way and that, twisted the pieces, tugged, and squished them together. No matter what he did, he couldn't get them apart.

At last Sir Ollen stood. "Thank you, young lady. You've been most helpful. Be assured we will hunt down and dispose of this monster."

"Oh, thank you," Hiera said, jumping to her feet. "Thank you."

"Great," Mudd said as soon as the knights walked out the door. "Let's get out of here."

"Right," Hiera said. "We need our things."

Drakecutter appeared at the top of the stairs. "Everything's packed."

"Where are the others?" Mudd asked. The smell of mince pies and boiled potatoes for lunch wafted in from the kitchen, and he hoped for a quick bite before they left.

"They went to buy more supplies," Drakecutter said. As he spoke, the inn door thumped open and Iroden entered, followed by Kirak carrying a heavy bundle of supplies on his back and a thick double-bladed battle-axe in his hands.

"Here," Kirak said, tossing the axe to Drakecutter. "You need a real weapon. You never know when you might be attacked out there in the mountains."

Drakecutter hefted the axe and took a few practice swings.

Mudd tensed. "Be careful with that thing."

Drakecutter laughed, and his eyes sparkled. "I've waited my whole life to plant an axe in some fell beast's gullet."

"Are we ready to go, then?" Kirak asked, readjusting the heavy bundle on his back.

"Yes," Mudd said. "Just as soon as we've eaten."

Hiera planted her hands on her hips and said to Kirak, "I can't believe you bought all this stuff."

"We'll need this gear, trust me," Kirak said. "I've been all over the Vingaard Mountains. This cave won't be easy to get to. Oh, don't look at me like that. I know you think you can scale a sheer cliff with just your fingernails, but the rest of us aren't rangers."

Mudd chuckled in agreement. He sat down to eat, anxious to be on their way to the cave.

~~~>➤~~~

Mudd hurried up the steep road away from Palanthas, part of him sad to leave behind the rush and excitement of the city, and part of him glad to be on their way. Hiera, Drakecutter, Iroden, and Kirak followed close behind.

"We're coming, Shemnara," Mudd muttered. "Just hold on."

They passed the guardhouse and forged up onto the Knight's High Road. The scent of pine wafted on the wind, whistling though the stately trees. Gray cliffs stretched up to mountain peaks above. Mudd wiped the sweat from his forehead after the long climb and took a drink of cold water.

Hiera lifted her face to the sunlight. "I'm glad to be out of the city. Too many people and buildings. No trees, no forest creatures, no soft dirt beneath your feet."

"You're crazy," Mudd said. "Palanthas is magnificent."

"I agree," Drakecutter said, running his fingers through his braided beard. "But we don't have time to stand around talking about it. We've already lost most of the day."

He struck out along the road as fast as his stout legs could go. Mudd and Hiera caught up within a few steps. Iroden had to run to stay with them. Kirak scooped him up under one lanky arm and kept pace with Mudd.

"Please," Iroden squeaked. "This is rather unbecoming."

Kirak chuckled and set him high up on his shoulders. "How's that?"

Iroden clutched at Kirak's long hair. "All right, I guess."

Mudd laughed, though he didn't know how Kirak could stand to carry the kender as well as his heavy pack. The extra weight didn't seem to bother Kirak, though.

"Kirak," Mudd said, giving him a warm smile. "Why do you think you were meant to find the dragon pendant?"

Kirak tensed. "Shemnara told me I was supposed to."

"Yes, of course." Mudd waved a placating hand. "I just thought perhaps you might have some idea. Most of the vision makes no sense. And then there are the pendant and the silver dragon. Why would the dragon want to grant someone a wish?"

Kirak frowned and fingered his sword hilts. "Silver dragons like humans. They want to help people. It's just their way."

Hiera came up on the other side of Kirak. "So when we find the pendant, what will you wish for, Kirak?"

Kirak's face darkened, and he dropped his gaze to the ground. "I don't know what I want anymore. Once I thought I would give anything to claim my true birthright. Now I would be happy if all of us just get out of this alive."

"You think it's that dangerous?" Mudd asked.

"There's a red dragon involved," Kirak said in a thick voice. "Of course there's danger. Red dragons are more cunning than you realize. I'll wager she didn't ravage your village and take Shemnara for no reason."

Mudd stopped in the road, his fist clenched. "Do you have some sort of idea why she might have done it?"

Kirak's face turned crimson. He sputtered, but no words came from his mouth.

"Oh, be reasonable, Mudd." Hiera patted Kirak's arm. "How should he know what the red dragon is up to any better than the rest of us? He just heard about it. We've had time to think and still haven't come up with anything."

"Sorry." Mudd hitched his pack up on his shoulders and started walking. The sun inched downward, casting long shadows across the road, and the wind turned cold.

"This whole thing is like an impenetrable lock," Mudd muttered. "I feel that if I just keep poking at it long enough it will spring open in my hands and I'll have the answer. Shemnara's gone, Drakecutter's axe taken, a red dragon, a silver dragon . . . I don't know."

"Perhaps a bit of dragon lore might be useful," Iroden said. "I have read many texts concerning dragons."

"Really?" Hiera beamed with excitement.

"Yes, really," Iroden smiled at her, his green eyes lighting up with pleasure at her response. "You see, red dragons make their lairs high in the mountains. They love to perch on cliffs overlooking their claimed territory. A silver dragon's domain is all the sky. They love to fly simply for the joy of it. It is rumored that they have enchanted lairs in the clouds with solid floors where they lay their eggs."

Kirak's eyes got a far away look for a moment, then his face went pale. "Get to the point, Iroden," he snapped.

Iroden jumped. "Well, the point is that red dragons and silver dragons both claim the same territory, which often brings them into mortal conflict with each other."

Kirak cleared his throat. "It will be dark soon. We'd better find a place to camp."

Mudd's mind whirled while he led them to the place where they'd camped on their way to Palanthas. Drakecutter got a fire going while Kirak and Iroden broke out the food from Kirak's pack. Mudd stood at the edge of their camp, staring up at the cliffs above them. His skin prickled with the thought that the red dragon could be up there somewhere, watching them.

Hiera slid over to Mudd, fingering her bow. "I've been thinking. What Iroden says makes sense, but there could be another explanation."

"What?" Mudd pulled out his puzzle and worried at it while Hiera talked.

"Set-ai said the Dark Queen, Takhisis, is always trying to take control of this world." Hiera looked around at the deepening shadows. "Just because she was defeated and forced back into the Abyss during the War of the Lance doesn't mean that she's given up on her designs."

"You think Takhisis sent the red dragon after Shemnara?" Mudd asked.

Hiera nodded. "She may have plans for a new war and doesn't want Shemnara warning anyone with her visions. She may not know Shemnara isn't a seer anymore."

"What about Drakecutter's axe?" Mudd clenched his fists. It was bad enough thinking about fighting a red dragon, but that was nothing compared to the Dark Queen.

"Stonefist used his axe to kill a lot of evil dragons during the war. The axe is too dangerous for the Dark Queen to leave in enemy hands." Hiera grimaced. "It's just an idea."

Mudd bit his lip. Before this all started, he would have sworn the only things Hiera thought about were how to make bread and which ribbons matched which dress. He'd always taken her for granted as his little sister. She'd studied hard with Set-ai, it seemed, and he hadn't even noticed that she'd grown into an intelligent and deadly ranger.

Hiera left him and went back to the fire to supervise the evening cooking. Mudd shook his head at how swiftly she changed from one role to the other. He just hoped she was up to the conflict that might lie ahead for them.

CHAPTER TWENTY-TWO

They set out again early the next morning while frost from the night's chill still clung to the trees. A flock of small gray birds whistled in the branches.

Mudd pulled his cloak tight around him and rubbed at his eyes. He hadn't slept well even after his turn at watch. A fiery red dragon haunted his dreams while the dark face of a beautiful and terrible woman laughed in the background. In his dream, only a thin ray of silver light had kept Mudd from the dragon's flames. He was glad when the sun came up to warm them with more natural light.

They traveled the High Road without much conversation. Mudd pushed them hard, fearing for Shemnara's life more than ever. Once in a while Drakecutter grumbled about the prolonged pace, but the others marched on without complaint. When Iroden grew tired, Kirak carried him. They reached the High Clerist's Tower by late afternoon.

Iroden stopped in the middle of the road and stared up at the structure. His hands twitched as if turning the pages of a book. "That's it, isn't it?" he said. "I've read all about it."

"Yes," Mudd said. "Come on." He pushed Iroden forward. Drakecutter was bad enough. Mudd didn't need Iroden to go goggle-eyed and slow down their progress too.

Iroden kept talking while he walked beside Mudd. "That tower rises over one thousand feet into the air. Its true name is Dragondeath."

Mudd gritted his teeth and hurried through the gate.

As they made their way across the central courtyard, Iroden pointed to the top of the towering wall in front of them. "That is the spot where the heroic knight Sturm Brightblade fell beneath the Dragon Highlord's spear."

Mudd's heart beat hard. Set-ai had told them stories about Sturm Brightblade. Sturm's heroic sacrifice had turned the tide of the war. Mudd was no knight, but if the Dark Queen were moving again in the world, he wondered if he would have the courage to stand against her minions as Sturm had. One thing was for sure: Mudd might have to face the red dragon and who-ever worked with her, be it Dragon Highlord or draconian.

Kirak grimaced and strode past Mudd out the gate. Mudd found him standing on the ramp that led down into the plains below. Kirak stared across the open fields with a bleak look on his face, his hands clenching his sword hilts.

"These plains are called the Wings of Habbakuk," Iroden said. "This is where the knights who would not listen to Sturm first rode forth against the dragonarmies. They died on the plains, every last one—"

Kirak jerked Iroden off the ground and shook him. "Let the dead sleep in peace." Kirak's voice was such a deep growl it almost didn't sound human. He dropped Iroden and marched down the ramp.

"What's wrong?" Hiera called and tried to run after him, but Mudd grabbed her arm.

"Leave him alone, Hiera," Mudd said. "Maybe he was a squire of one of the knights who died here."

Mudd glanced at Drakecutter and imagined the bloodthirsty draconians who had lured the knights into the trap on the plains and then killed them. Drakecutter stared at the empty fields below, but Mudd couldn't see any evil lurking in his eyes.

Mudd followed Kirak down the ramp onto the bright spring grass. During the war, whole armies had struggled to bring freedom to Solamnia. He didn't have an army to free Shemnara, but he had to find a way.

With Hiera leading, they skirted the tower and headed up the mountain slopes to the east. The map showed the way up a steep rock slide and over a jagged pass into the mountains beyond.

The sun was near setting by the time they struggled to the top of the pass. Mudd's lungs burned. He gasped in the thin air. A cold wind whipped the mountainside. If he weren't sweating so hard from the exertion of climbing, he might have pulled out his cloak to keep warm.

He came to a rock slide of rough shale that ended at the tree line below. The rocks slipped and clattered beneath his feet, and Mudd struggled to keep from sliding down. Drakecutter used the haft of his axe to stay upright.

Hiera leaped onto the shale with a cry of delight and slid toward the trees, keeping her footing somehow in the spray of rocks and dirt. Her lithe figure seemed to dance down the mountainside.

"Hiera, you're crazy," Mudd said, scrambling down after her. Kirak, Drakecutter, and Iroden followed with more care.

"What took you so long?" she said with a coy grin once they'd all joined her.

Mudd laughed.

Hiera pulled out the map and stared at it for a moment, then led them down into the forest.

Shadows deepened around them. The wind continued to blow, giving life to the trees, which swayed and groaned, rattling leaves and pine needles.

"We better find a place to camp," Mudd said. "It's probably not safe stumbling around the mountain in the dark."

Hiera stopped in a level clearing and let her pack slip to the ground. "Keep the fire small," she ordered. "We don't know what might be out here."

The forest brooded around them while they ate dinner. Mudd finished off his portion of salted pork, gobbled some bread and cheese, then inched closer to the fire and pulled out the gnomes' puzzle he had yet to solve.

Hiera eased over to Iroden. "Now that we've told you everything about the silver dragon and the pendant, would you like to tell us how you became a kender?"

"Why should I?" Iroden said, poking the fire with a stick. "You won't believe me anyway."

Hiera wrapped her arm around his slender shoulders. "Maybe the others don't believe you're really an elf, but I do. I trust you, Iroden, and you can trust me."

Mudd looked up from his puzzle, curious to see what the kender would say. Drakecutter snorted and laid out his bedroll by the fire. Kirak grimaced.

Iroden stabbed the fire with his stick, sending up a shower of sparks and a puff of smoke that blew in Mudd's face. Mudd coughed and licked his lips. The taste of burnt pine stayed on his tongue.

Hiera waited quietly for Iroden to speak.

Iroden took a deep breath. "I was attending to my clerical duties late one evening. It was dark, and I was almost home when I saw two older clerics hurrying down the road. Their business was none of my affair. I would have continued on my way, but—"

An owl hooted in the dark branches above them. Iroden paused and pursed his lips.

"Go on," Hiera encouraged him.

"I heard a muffled cry from something bulky carried beneath one of the cleric's robes," Iroden continued. "A dark fear came over me, and I followed them. They led me into a thick grove of aspen trees where branches huddled together and dense underbrush made the way difficult.

"At last they came out into a clearing, and I hunched down behind an elderberry bush, watching. The clerics lit two candles and set them on either end of a black marble altar. At the head of the altar hunched a fat statue with cold eyes and an oily smile."

Kirak sucked in a sharp breath. "Hiddukel!"

"You've heard of the evil god?" Iroden asked, surprised.

Kirak let out a low laugh. "I've known too much evil in my life. They say that Hiddukel is the only being that can make a deal with the Dark Queen and come out ahead. He's full of mischief and controls all ill-gotten wealth."

Iroden nodded, the light and shadow from the fire making his gaunt face look menacing. "One of the clerics drew forth a bound elf child from beneath his cloak and tied the boy to the altar. I froze in shock as they chanted a vile prayer to Hiddukel. These were the same clerics who in broad daylight had taken vows to serve E'li. They were going to sacrifice the child in exchange for being made royalty. In some twisted way, they thought they could gain the kingdom's treasures for themselves."

Iroden shuddered. His hand shook on the stick, and he dropped it into the fire. Mudd found himself clutching the puzzle so tightly it pressed into his palm.

"A deep laugh filled the clearing," Iroden whispered. "And a cloud of darkness poured from Hiddukel's mouth, covering the altar. The boy screamed, and I rushed forward from my hiding place. I fumbled to untie the child from the altar, but one of the clerics grabbed me from behind."

Hiera gasped. "But what happened to the child? How did you get free?"

"I smashed the cleric in the face with my fist. He let go just long enough for me to free the boy and tell him to run. Then they both had their hands on me. All the while Hiddukel laughed. One of the clerics drew out a dagger and lifted it over my heart."

Iroden fell silent. The fire crackled. Smoke lifted up between the pine branches above.

Mudd clamped his mouth shut and stared at the burning embers. As much as he wanted to hear the end of the story, he couldn't bring himself to urge Iroden on with the tale.

Mudd put another log onto the fire. Iroden's dark story made him shudder, and he wished for more light despite Hiera's warning to keep the fire small. The flames licked skyward with a comforting yellow glow.

"But they didn't kill you?" Kirak asked Iroden, urging him to continue.

"No." Iroden's voice shook. "Hiddukel stopped them. He said I deserved worse than death. Then he cursed me. I cannot describe the pain. It seemed to go on forever. When it stopped, one of the clerics grabbed my robes and lifted me into the air. My feet swung back and forth above the ground. I had become a kender."

"And then what happened? Didn't anyone believe you?" Hiera asked, still huddling near the kender.

"The clerics beat me and threw me out of the city without

any word to my father. No one knew, no one who could help me. It took me a long time to get to Palanthas, but I was sure Revered Son Elistan could help me regain my true form." Iroden sighed and put his head between his hands. "I was wrong."

Mudd jumped to his feet and stepped away from the fire. "I'll take first watch." Iroden's tale made his soul shiver. What if it were true? Mudd pushed the idea aside. He didn't want to think about anything so heinous. The night was dark enough already without that.

CHAPTER TWENTY-THREE

Mudd woke stiff and cold the next morning. They ate a hurried breakfast and set out again without speaking much. Hiera led them through the dense underbrush and tall pine trees. Mudd shivered in the shadows. A squirrel eyed him from a branch above, then darted into its hole. A flock of birds took flight, screaming.

A sour taste lingered on Mudd's tongue. Pine needles snapped beneath his boots. After hiking for a while they came out of the trees and into a narrow meadow where mountain bluebells and delicate asters rustled in the long grass.

Except for the wind blowing through the flowers, a deep silence hung over the valley. Though the sun shone overhead, a dark worry tugged at Mudd's consciousness. He tensed.

Hiera frowned. "I don't like the look of this." She hovered among the trees, reluctant to step into the open.

"What's the matter?" Drakecutter asked. "I don't see anything out there except those useless flowers."

"Exactly," Hiera said. "The forest animals have gone silent, and a meadow like that should be buzzing with hummingbirds and butterflies."

Mudd glanced up at the sky. "Maybe the dragon's close by?"

"Could be, but I don't feel it," Hiera said. "I think we should stay out of the meadow anyway."

She led them around the edge of it, staying beneath the tall pine trees that covered the slopes.

Here and there thick patches of snow still clung to the dark places that never saw sunlight. Freezing water seeped out from the snow, leaving the ground muddy. Though Mudd and the others had come off the pass, the air was still thin and cold.

Mudd rubbed his hand against a tree, and sticky pine gum clung to his fingers. He tried to wipe it off on his trousers but only succeeded in spreading it around. His mind strayed to the time he'd traveled with Hector, and his hand went to the puzzle in his pocket. Hector could have thought of some invention for getting pine gum off.

"Mudd." Hiera's whisper surprised him.

He turned to look back and realized he'd gotten ahead of the others. They stood around Hiera, who knelt beside a patch of muddy ground, created by a tall snowbank that huddled against the curve of the mountain.

"What is it?" he asked, taking a step back toward them.

"Shh," Hiera hissed. "I'd say large wolf tracks, except wolves don't walk on two feet."

A guttural roar interrupted Hiera's speculations. Five hairy creatures that looked like a cross between hyenas and men leaped from behind the snowbank. They wore ragged mail armor that had been haphazardly pieced together. Each carried a large shield and a wicked axe with blades that topped both ends of the haft.

"Gnolls!" Hiera cried.

Mudd swore and reached for his bow.

The gnolls charged at Hiera and the others, their clawed feet kicking up the snow as they raced across it. Hiera whipped out her knives, Kirak drew his swords, and Drakecutter set his stance with his axe clutched in his hands.

Iroden yelped in fear and raced past Mudd out into the meadow.

Mudd snorted in amusement at Iroden and shot an arrow at the gnoll that led the attack. The arrow pinged off its shield. Before Mudd could loose another shot, a great weight fell on him, driving him to his knees. A gnoll had leaped from a tree branch above to land on him.

The stench of wet fur gagged Mudd as the gnoll buried its sharp teeth in his shoulder. Mudd screamed, thrashing to get his hand free and pull his dagger out of the sheath.

The creature clung to Mudd's back, keeping him pressed against the ground so he couldn't get a clear strike at it. Mudd stabbed awkwardly over his shoulder at the gnoll's face. His dagger sunk into its eye.

The gnoll unclamped its jaws from Mudd's shoulder to bellow in outrage. Mudd twisted out from underneath it and drew his sword just in time to block the creature's wild axe swing.

Metal clanged against metal as the two weapons met in the air. The impact drove Mudd back to his knees.

Behind him, Drakecutter screamed a battle cry, and the thunk of axe tearing through flesh filled the air.

The gnoll Mudd fought shoved its shield in Mudd's face. Mudd twisted away and swung his sword at the gnoll's neck. The gnoll blocked at the same time it jabbed the bottom end of its weapon at Mudd's stomach.

Mudd danced back and swung again. His sword clanked off the gnoll's armor, the vibration of the impact shivering Mudd's hand.

A glimpse of the rest of the battle showed that Drakecutter had felled one gnoll and was close to finishing off a second while Hiera fought two others. Her blades swished in silver streaks, blocking, jabbing, spinning.

Kirak stabbed the gnoll he fought through the chest, and it thumped to the ground at his feet. He leaped at the gnolls attacking Hiera.

The gnoll Mudd fought swung its axe, and Mudd ducked. The sharp blade sang past his ear. Mudd's sword hilt grew slick with the blood that trickled down from the bite on his shoulder. He blocked blow after blow, but because of the bite, didn't have the strength in his arm to strike the gnoll very hard.

"Look out. There's three more," Hiera cried.

"I got them," both Kirak and Drakecutter said at the same time.

Mudd couldn't spare the effort to look over his shoulder

and make sure his friends were still all right. The only things keeping him alive were concentration and agility.

He tripped over his fallen bow and tumbled to his knees. The gnoll sprang forward, swinging its axe at Mudd. Mudd rolled away and got back to his feet.

Block. Strike. Dodge. His shoulder throbbed. The creature squinted at him with one bloody eye, the other flaming yellow. Saliva dripped from its sharp teeth.

"Ha! I got one," Hiera yelled.

Another raced at her. She backed up against a tree near where Mudd was fighting, drawing Mudd's attention.

Her knives flashed between the gnoll's axe strokes, cutting at its exposed lower arm and wrist. She hooked one of her blades up behind its shield and cut its hand.

It dropped the shield with a feral scream.

A fiery pain cut across Mudd's sword arm. He'd missed a dodge while watching Hiera. His hand went limp, and his sword fell to the ground.

The gnoll's axe swung again. Mudd twisted away, but the axe cut across his stomach as he tried to distance himself from his attacker. Mudd cried out and gripped his dagger in his good hand. The gnoll snarled and lunged at him. The fire of victory gleamed in its eye.

Mudd stepped to the side and slipped in beneath the gnoll's arm, stabbing his dagger into the gnoll's neck. For a moment he thought it wouldn't pierce the gnoll's tough skin. Screaming, he put all his weight into it.

It worked. The gnoll gave a gurgling cry and fell. Mudd fell with it, tangled up between the gnoll's shield and arms.

He thrashed away from the fallen gnoll and leaped to his feet, his hand pressed against the wound in his stomach. Hiera still battled her gnoll, but it was sluggish from loss of blood. Its blows were wild, and Hiera dodged them with a grim smile.

Mudd's vision swam, and he fell to his knees.

Kirak wielded his heavy swords with grim determination. Two gnolls lay at his feet, and a third looked ready to join them. Drakecutter dropped his gnoll with a final swing of his axe.

A faint rustle above Hiera in the tree caught Mudd's attention. He looked up to see a gnoll leap from the branches toward his sister just at the moment that she buried her knives in the other gnoll's chest.

"Hiera!" Mudd cried. But even as he yelled, he knew his warning would be too late.

Kirak turned and pointed at Hiera's attacker.

The gnoll stopped in midair, its feet barely off the branch. No, "stopped" wasn't the right word. It was still falling toward Hiera, but slowly, like a feather adrift on the wind.

Hiera tore her knives free from the gnoll in front of her and waited while the confused gnoll above her floated into range.

Whoosh whoosh. Her knives struck, killing the gnoll. It drifted to the ground and landed softly at her feet.

Kirak raced over to her. The rest of the gnolls had fallen—three killed by Kirak, three by Drakecutter, and three by Hiera.

Mudd looked at the one sorry gnoll he'd killed. Black specks swam across his vision. "I'd rather pick a lock any day," he muttered before collapsing.

Chapter Twenty-Four

Mudd lay on the ground, clutching his stomach. Hiera's blurry face leaned over him. Her forehead wrinkled with worry.

"Drakecutter," she yelled. "Mudd's hurt. Go find Iroden."

While Drakecutter lumbered away, Hiera pressed a swath of material against Mudd's stomach and tied others around the wounds in his arm and shoulder.

Kirak stood guard above them, his swords out in case any more gnolls appeared.

"Hiera." Mudd struggled to speak. The gash in his arm might heal if it were stitched and bandaged, but he knew the wound in his stomach would not. He gulped short gasps of air.

"Shhh. Don't talk, Mudd. You'll be fine." Hiera wiped his face with a damp cloth.

"No, Hiera. Promise me you'll finish the quest even without me. Find the pendant and save Shemnara." The world spun, and Mudd squeezed his eyes shut.

"I'm not going anywhere without you," Hiera said. "Don't even think about dying."

"Move aside. Let me see him." Iroden's voice sounded far away, but his tiny, warm hand pressed against Mudd's chest.

"Hold on, Mudd," he said. "Just for a little while." Iroden started a musical chant in a flowing language that might have been Elvish. Mudd recognized only one word, E'li, Iroden's name for Paladine. Still believing himself a cleric, Iroden was calling on his god to heal Mudd.

Mudd almost laughed, but he didn't have the strength. Seconds stretched on while he struggled to keep breathing. A comfortable warmth spread through his body. His stomach and arm tingled.

He gasped, and sweet mountain air rushed into his lungs. The pain of his wounds vanished.

Hiera squealed with joy, and Mudd blinked. Iroden knelt beside him, still clutching Paladine's medallion in his hand. His face glowed with golden radiance, though the glow faded as Mudd watched.

Mudd touched his stomach and found tender new skin beneath his hand.

Iroden patted Mudd's arm. "You'll be all right now."

Mudd swallowed and looked up into Iroden's small kender face. "You really are a Silvanesti cleric, aren't you? I'm sorry I doubted."

Iroden gave him a grim smile. "You believed enough to invite me to come with you."

"And I'm glad I did." Mudd forced his reluctant body to sit.

He saw that while Iroden had healed him, Drakecutter had scraped out a shallow hole in the mud and dragged the dead gnolls into it. Now he worked to cover the bodies. Soil clung to his hands and axe.

He finished with a final grunt. "I've dug dirt and put seeds into the ground all my life. But nothing will grow from this garden." He frowned at the mound of dirt while he brushed the mud off his hands.

"Mudd will need food and a good rest before we go on," Iroden told Hiera.

"We can't stay here," Kirak said. "There may be more gnolls about."

Mudd looked up at Kirak. His thin body belied his great strength. The heavy swords he held in either hand would have been difficult for Mudd to wield even using both hands.

After Kirak's performance during the battle, Mudd was even more convinced he'd been some great knight's squire. But that didn't account for the bit of magic Kirak had done slowing the gnoll's fall from the tree.

"Are you a wizard?" Mudd asked. "I saw you cast some kind of spell to stop the gnoll from jumping on Hiera."

Kirak flushed. "Not a wizard. Not really. Some things just come naturally to me."

"What else can you do?" Hiera asked. She stroked Mudd's forehead, dividing her attention between her brother and Kirak.

"Not much. I can only do that slow fall thing you saw.

Pfeatherfall, I think some call it. And I can make it foggy. Sometimes I can get the wind to do what I want, like blow flames away from my face and such." Kirak glanced around them. "We really should get moving. This isn't a safe spot."

Hiera helped Mudd to his feet. "Can you walk?"

Mudd nodded. "I think so." His legs threatened to give out.

"Here." Iroden gave him a drink of water and several strips of smoked beef. "You've got to eat something even if we can't rest here."

Mudd thanked him and chewed on the beef while they set off again. The food gave him a measure of renewed strength.

Hiera led them out of the valley and up another steep trail. It switched back and forth across the mountain face, going up and up for what seemed like forever.

Mudd grew light-headed and struggled to stay with the others. The trail rose so steep he had to use his hands to help pull himself upward. Giant boulders littered the incline, making the climb treacherous as he moved from one rock to the next. Nothing grew that high up except for an occasional columbine down between the rocks. Scores of spiderwebs hung glistening between boulders. Green and black striped spiders scurried out of view as Mudd climbed over them.

They came to a cliff that rose twenty feet high. The setting sun painted the cold rock red as Mudd paused to catch his breath.

Kirak pulled his pack off his shoulder and rummaged

inside. Mudd stared at the cliff, doubting he could climb it even with Kirak's gear.

Hiera pulled out the map. "Looks like the cave is just on the other side of this peak."

Kirak nodded. "This cliff is probably the last obstacle in the way. Looks like from up there we'll be able to skirt around the peak and head down the other side."

"No problem," Mudd said, gritting his teeth. Though he didn't feel much pain, the exhaustion of the healing and the climbing had caught up to him. "We'll be there in no time."

If the jagged cliff face had a voice, it would have laughed.

CHAPTER TWENTY-FIVE

Hiera glanced at Mudd, then took the rope from Kirak's hands. "It's nearly dark," she said. "Too late to start climbing now. See that alcove there where the cliff juts out from the mountain? It should give us enough shelter to camp for the night."

Mudd frowned, but he was too weak to argue. It galled him that they were so close to the cave with the pendant, but they had to stop for him. He knew he was lucky to be alive. And he owed that to Iroden.

A funny feeling made his stomach squirm as he looked from Hiera, who resolutely led them to the alcove; to Iroden, who kept glancing up the cliff face with frightened eyes; to Kirak, who scanned the tree line below for any sign of threat; and to Drakecutter, who slumped against a rock and used his dagger to clean the mud from beneath his fingernails.

Mudd had intended to go after the pendant alone, and now they all stood with him. He had to admit he would have gotten this far without the others. Still, a warning v[nagged at him.

He slid into the alcove and pulled the puzzle out of his pocket. He'd never encountered anything so aggravating. Every other lock and puzzle he'd been able to figure out in no time. But this one refused to come apart, no matter how he twisted and tugged at it.

Hiera slung her pack off her back. "We shouldn't risk a fire."

Drakecutter snorted. "Good, because I'm not climbing all the way back down to the tree line to haul firewood up here."

The others crowded into the alcove and spread out their bedrolls.

"I'll take first watch." Kirak positioned himself at the front of the alcove.

Mudd gobbled more beef and a few hard biscuits from his pack. Hiera pulled out her red box. The lacquer glimmered in the setting sun, and the glass flashed as she opened it out to form a mirror.

She washed her face and loosened her hair from the bun. The blonde waves fell down around her shoulders, and she stroked them with the comb.

Kirak stared at her in admiration. Hiera didn't seem to notice. Though Mudd had seen it before, her transformation astonished him. One moment she was a hardened ranger, and the next a beautiful young woman. The strong hands that had felled three gnolls tenderly gripped the comb with graceful fingers.

Mudd couldn't blame Kirak for staring, but he didn't like it either. "I thought you were watching for gnolls," he snapped.

Kirak started. His silver eyes rested on Hiera for a half a second longer, then he turned his back and stared down the mountain.

"Well, aren't you grumpy," Hiera said.

When Mudd was still quite young, his father had told him it would be his job to look after his younger sister, especially when she started to have suitors. Mudd had figured that would never happen.

Iroden smiled at Hiera. "You are very lovely for a human. If you were an elf, I might. . . ." His face colored. "Well, Mudd might be snapping at me too."

Hiera lowered her comb. "What are you talking about?"

Iroden ducked and made a show of fishing around in his pack.

Mudd shook his head and reached for Hiera's mirror while she glared at Iroden, perplexed.

Hinges held the pieces of the mirror together so they could fold up into the cube, but Mudd found he could swing the hinges either way and create other shapes with the glass. He folded it this way and that, experimenting until Hiera slapped his hands and took it away.

"What is Iroden talking about?" she whispered to him.

"You're not a little girl anymore," Mudd said. "I guess I hadn't noticed, but you've grown up a bit. I think Kirak likes you."

Hiera gasped and put the comb and mirror away. "That's ridiculous."

"I agree," Mudd whispered. "For the record, I'm not going to let you court anyone until you're twenty."

She slugged him in the arm. "I'll court whom and when I want."

Mudd winced. She'd hit him close to where the wound had been, and his arm was still a bit tender.

Iroden frowned. "It should feel better in the morning. You must rest for a healing like that to take full effect."

The next morning Mudd did feel much stronger. He got up and stretched. A layer of frost clung to the ground and the cliff rocks. The sun shone off the intricate frosty patterns, making them look like the guts inside a gnomish invention.

They ate breakfast and packed up, eager to get an early start over the mountain. Mudd flexed his arm, testing it before going up the cliff. It seemed fine.

"I'll go first," Kirak said. He started up the cliff.

Mudd followed, catching a handhold in a crevice above his head. The rock was sharp and crumbly beneath his fingertips. Inch by inch he made his way up.

Kirak reached the top and secured a rope, which he threw down to the others. Hiera and Mudd reached the top at the same time a moment later. Only Drakecutter and Iroden remained below

Drakecutter caught hold of the rope and hauled himself up hand over hand.

"Come on, Iroden," Mudd called.

Iroden looked down at the steep mountain slope below him,

and then up the cliff face. "I don't think I can do it," he said.

"Just climb the rope," Hiera said. "You're not afraid of heights, are you?"

"I never thought about it before," Iroden shouted up to them. "But now that it comes to it, yes, I think I am."

Drakecutter snorted. Kirak grimaced, and Hiera rolled her eyes.

"Just tie the rope around your middle and we'll haul you up," Mudd called down.

Iroden drew the end of the rope around his waist and fumbled to tie it. As soon as it looked like it would hold, Kirak pulled him up.

"Ouch. Oh!" Iroden cried as he bounced and scraped up the cliff. When he reached the top, he spread himself flat on the ground and refused to move.

"It's all right," Hiera said, kneeling beside him and stroking his back.

"By Reorx's beard, get up," Drakecutter said. "We're almost there."

Mudd tried to ignore the eager glint in Drakecutter's eye. He reached down, picked Iroden up, and set him on his feet away from the edge. Iroden brushed the dirt and rock splinters off his clothes, his expression grim.

Wind tugged at Mudd's hair. The mountain peak towered above him like a great bald stone head. Leading the others, Mudd skirted around the peak and started down the other side. An apron of boulders stretched out below them, down and down and down. About halfway down, a finger of blackness stood amid the rocks.

"That's it," Mudd said. "Let's go."

He scrambled over the rocks, eager to get into the cave and find the pendant.

"Wait for us," Hiera said, coming down behind him.

Mudd hesitated at the cave's mouth. Cool, damp air wafted out. The opening was narrow, barely big enough for one person to fit at a time. Water dripped somewhere in the darkness below.

"It sure doesn't look like much," Kirak said.

Iroden gripped his medallion and mumbled a prayer to E'li.

Drakecutter took a deep breath. "Finally, I get to go underground. I know it's not Thorbardin or anything like that, but at least it's a cave. Imagine a dwarf living his whole life above ground. It's not natural."

"Your father seems to like living above ground and farming," Kirak said.

Drakecutter flushed.

Kirak laughed. He lit two small lanterns and handed one to Mudd. "Do you want to go first, or shall I?"

"I'll go first," Mudd said. He lifted the lantern and eased into the dark hole.

CHAPTER TWENTY-SIX

The lantern threw jagged fingers of light on the damp walls that rose up on either side of Mudd. Water dripped in the darkness ahead. Sharp stones littered the ground. Mudd sucked in a breath of the heavy wet air and stepped farther into the cave.

"Look at that," Hiera said.

Mudd lowered the lantern to where she pointed. A hole near the wall dropped down into blackness.

"Stay on the path," Mudd said, "and stay close together. One wrong step into something like that and you'll be dead." His voice echoed back at them from the darkness below.

Hiera's face grew pale, and she put a shaking hand on Mudd's arm. "I don't like it in here."

Mudd grinned. "I haven't had so much fun since I snuck into the mayor's wine cellar."

"You did what?" Hiera squeaked. "Why?"

Mudd laughed. "I think I'd better keep that to myself." He moved forward again, testing each step before putting a foot down. That close to the edge of nothingness, the rock could give way without warning.

After a time, the narrow corridor opened up into a sandy chamber. Mudd surveyed the room, noting signs that it had been occupied at one time. A pile of rags sat in the shadows against one wall. A pot with a rusted hole lay on its side. A black circle marked the ground where a fire had been lit.

Hiera sucked in a breath. "Nobody move," she said. "Give me the lantern."

Mudd handed her the lantern, and she lowered it to inspect the thick sand on the ground. Everyone waited in silence.

"Gnolls," Hiera whispered. "I think this might have been their lair." She eased over to the fire pit and tested the coals. "This fire has been lit more recently than when that mercenary Mudd read about at the library was here."

Kirak handed his lantern to Iroden and drew his swords. Drakecutter swung his axe and glared around the room. Hiera unsheathed her knives.

Three passageways led out from the chamber: the one they'd come in by, and two others. One of them was a wide path with a rocky floor. The other was jagged and narrow like the one they'd just come through.

"How old would you say the tracks are?" Kirak asked.

"I can't tell," Hiera said. "There isn't any wind or weather to wear them down. I can see the mercenaries' footprints faintly in the dust here and there beneath the gnolls'. The fire's been out for several days."

"Let's hope we killed the whole pack of them," Mudd said. "Be ready just the same."

He walked over to the narrow passage and lifted the lantern, hoping to see some sign of which one he should take. "Does the map say which way we should go from here?"

Hiera shook her head.

"Look at this." Kirak pointed high up on the walls at the start of the wider passage. Two shallow scratches marred the rock on either side.

"Why do you suppose the gnolls did that?" Hiera asked.

"They couldn't have," Kirak said. "It's too high up. Those look like they were made by dragon scales scraping the rock."

"I guess we go this way," Mudd said.

They followed the passage deeper into the mountain. It slanted downward and widened. Mudd's boots crunched against the rocks. His right arm started to ache from holding the lantern up, and he switched to use his left. Water dripped from the walls, making the air smell musty. Mineral deposits rippled like ruffles on the bottom of a rich lady's dress. Stalactites jutted down from the ceiling. Water dripped from their tips, forming jawlike stalagmites on the ground below them.

A dark gap loomed up in front of Mudd. Light refused to reflect out of it. He checked his lamp to see if it had gone out, but the flame still burned.

He took a step toward the gap, and Hiera grabbed the back of his shirt. "Mudd, don't," she cried. Her voice echoed around them.

He held the lantern out and leaned forward. His mind reeled, and he jumped back. What he'd taken for mere darkness was in fact a chasm so wide and so deep the light could not penetrate to the bottom or other side.

"Great," Drakecutter said. "I guess we took the wrong path."

"No, I don't think so," Iroden said, speaking for the first time since they entered the cave. He pointed to a set of flowing runes inscribed in the stone wall behind them.

Mudd moved his lantern closer for a better look. They were similar to the ones on the arch in Shemnara's vision. "What do they say?" he asked Iroden.

Iroden shook his head. "We should go back. There must be some better way."

"Read it for us," Hiera urged. "Then we can decide."

Iroden swallowed. His voice shook as he spoke. "'He who has courage must jump into the void.'"

"What kind of stupid saying is that?" Drakecutter grumbled. Kirak knelt at the edge and peered down into the darkness.

"It's a test," Mudd said. "The test of courage. We're on the right track." He pulled out a rope and tied it to a stalagmite.

"What are you doing?" Hiera grabbed the rope.

Mudd wiggled it out of her grasp and secured the opposite end around his waist. "I'm being courageous."

He kissed her cheek and dived off the edge and into the darkness.

CHAPTER TWENTY-SEVEN

Mudd's stomach leaped up to his heart as his feet left the solid ground behind him. He hung suspended over the chasm for a moment, one hand clutching the rope and the other holding the lantern.

Then he fell, but not in the direction he'd planned to go.

Instead of dropping feet first into the chasm, blood rushed to his head as if he were hanging upside down, and he launched upward.

He cried out in surprise, a wild exhilaration filling him. It wasn't like flying, though. He had no control. He tumbled upward into the darkness and became disoriented.

He rose at an alarming rate. Though his mind told him he was going up, his body felt like he was going down, speeding to a rocky death.

Sharp stalactites came into view. He rushed toward them. The rope remained slack in his hand. It was too long and would not snap tight before he slammed into the deadly points.

"Kirak!" Mudd yelled. "Stop me!"

Below him Kirak laughed. The sharp rock points raced at Mudd's face and chest like an army of spears.

Mudd slowed and floated gently to the stalactites. He twisted to avoid the points and came to rest against the surface. His head swam. He lay at the top of the cave just the same as if he were lying on the ground.

"Mudd!" Hiera called to him. "Are you all right?"

"Yes," Mudd answered. He stood, brushed himself off, and gazed above him down to the others below. He couldn't see them. The lantern's light did not reach far enough up into the darkness—or *down* into the darkness, Mudd wasn't sure which.

"This is too strange," he muttered. A faint silver glow in one of the stalactites caught his attention.

"It's called reverse gravity," Kirak shouted to him. "A silver dragon trick. I saw them use it to fight the dragonarmies during the war."

Mudd couldn't help smiling as he pictured hordes of draconians flung into the air where the dragons could snatch them up in their jaws or freeze them with a cone of cold air and send them tumbling back down to their deaths.

"So you did fight in the war," Mudd called down while he made his way to the glowing stalactite. "I thought you might have been a squire."

Mudd pried the glowing object from the damp stone. It was a small piece of silver a quarter the size of his palm. It pulsed with silver light and warmed his hand.

As soon as it came free, Mudd fell, yelping.

Wind rushed past him, tearing at his face and clothes as he plunged back down toward the others and the chasm below.

"Kirak!" Mudd screamed. "I'm falling."

He slowed, making his stomach flip-flop. Sliding the silver piece into his pocket, he held the lantern out to look for any sign of the far edge of the chasm.

Below him, the others came into view, staring up at him from the chasm's side.

Mudd twisted in the air and swam away from them. Batting his arms, kicking his legs, and tumbling sideways as he floated down, he managed to cross the chasm. Gradually the other side came into view. He did a slow flip in the air and landed with his feet on the hard, reassuring stone.

He grinned. His heart thudded with excitement. After it was all over, he'd have to convince Kirak to let him practice falling like that from the top of what remained of Karac-Tor, the mountain near Potter's Mill.

He tied off the rope to a stalagmite. With a lantern on both sides of the chasm, Mudd could see across to where the others stood.

"Come on over," he called.

Iroden yelped.

"Don't worry," Kirak said, putting a hand on Iroden's shoulder. "I'll make sure you don't fall." He tied Iroden against his chest, then swung down onto the rope and made his way across, hand over hand. Iroden kept his eyes squeezed shut and moaned all the way over.

Drakecutter followed. Clinging to the rope with his hands and looping his knees overtop as well, he shimmied slowly across.

Hiera went last, swinging across as Kirak had done. Her face was red, and she gasped for air by the time Mudd grabbed her and helped her onto safe ground.

While she recovered her breath, Mudd pulled out the glowing silver piece and lifted it so they could see the tiny curved object. "I think it's part of a key."

"Part of a key?" Kirak frowned at him.

"Yes," Mudd said. "It's like the metal's been splintered somehow. The question is: What happened to the rest of the key?"

"How do you know it's a key?" Drakecutter asked, squinting at the tiny piece of silver.

Hiera smiled. "Mudd knows a lot more about locks and keys than he does about fighting gnolls."

Mudd grimaced and slid the key into his pocket.

The passage they'd been following continued, though the ceiling lowered so Kirak had to stoop to get through. Mudd just had to duck his head. He'd grown a bit in the last few years, but he was still small for his age.

Hiera eased through behind him. "Mudd, I don't like these tests," she said. "If that was just the first one, how bad do you think the others will be?"

"I'm sure they'll be great," Mudd said with a laugh. "I've never had so much fun in my life."

"I should have guessed you'd say that," Hiera said, slapping his back.

Despite his lightheartedness, Mudd grew tense at the thought of the next test. Hiera was right about the danger. If Kirak hadn't been with them, Mudd would have died.

The top of the cave dropped lower, forcing Mudd to hunch over to continue. Cold water dripped on his face from the rocks only inches above him. He held the lamp out with one hand and gripped his sword hilt with the other. Only one mercenary had survived the path into the mountain, and they were skilled soldiers.

A faint noise sounded from the cave ahead.

Mudd stopped and motioned for the others to be quiet.

The noise came again amid the sound of water dripping—a quiet chink of metal against metal, like chains rattling.

"I don't like the sound of that," Hiera whispered.

Mudd agreed but continued forward, his curiosity piqued. Besides, the only other choice was to turn back, and he could never let Shemnara down like that. Whatever tests lay ahead, he had to be ready to take them.

The sound of chains grew louder, drifting to him intermittently as he crept forward. Soon muffled sobbing joined the whisper of chains and the plink of water.

The passage opened up into a small muddy cavern, and Mudd's eyes fell on a horrible sight. He froze with the lantern held in his hand as the others stepped out beside him.

Chapter Twenty-Eight

Kirak stepped into the cavern, his boots squelching on the muddy floor. The scent of fear and human waste filled the room, reminding him of the old days in the dragon army. He grimaced, guessing the source of the smell before he saw it.

"Slaves," he said.

Brutal iron chains held six small children against the far wall. Their clothes were in tatters, and their bodies were filthy. Their skin stretched tight over fragile bones. A blue light shimmered around the chains that held them.

Kirak shuddered.

"How could there be slaves here?" Drakecutter boomed.

"Gnolls almost always keep slaves," Kirak said, though gnolls weren't the only foul creatures to do so.

Hiera rushed forward. "We have to help them."

"Wait." Kirak grabbed her. "The chains have some kind of enchantment on them."

The blue light flashed, and a ragged girl screamed in pain.

A toddler at her feet cried soundlessly, his voice gone and tears dried up.

"Kirak, we have to do something," Hiera said. She tried to pull away from him.

"Of course we do." Kirak shoved her into Mudd's arms and strode forward, drawing his swords.

"Don't kill us!" a boy with a gaunt face and hopeless eyes screamed.

"I'm not going to hurt you," Kirak said. "I'm just going to cut the chains." He hoped that was possible. There was no telling what kind of enchantment lay on them. But as he looked into the children's faces, he felt their pain, their fear, and their hunger. His heart screamed out that he must help them.

He swung both swords together at the top of the chain near where it was attached to the wall. A bright light flashed just before his blades made contact with the iron. The swords flew from his hands.

Hiera and Mudd ducked just in time to avoid them as they whizzed overhead, clattered against the far wall, and fell to the ground.

Mudd straightened and pulled out a small black bundle. "Let me handle this, Kirak."

Kirak stepped away. His arms tingled from the force of the shock that had struck the swords from his hands.

The children whimpered as Mudd knelt next to the toddler and inserted a set of lock picks into one of the manacles. The light flashed again, sending Mudd sprawling.

Kirak shook his head and retrieved his swords while Mudd fished along the dirty ground to regain his lock picks.

"Look at this," Iroden said. His voice quivered. He stood next to the wall beside the passage they'd come from. His fingers traced another set of runes carved into the stone.

"What does it say?" Mudd asked.

Iroden's eyes grew wide and his hands shook. He read the runes. "It says, 'To free the captives you must have love enough to take their place.'"

Kirak swallowed.

"Look there," Iroden said, pointing to the wall next to the children. An empty pair of manacles hung beside the little girl.

"I don't like the sound of that," Mudd said.

Tears sprang into Hiera's eyes. "We have to do something. We can't just leave them like this."

"Help us," the little girl pleaded. The others who were old enough to talk joined in her cries. "Save us. Please."

Kirak wiped his swords clean and sheathed them. The dragon pendant hid somewhere in the cave, waiting for him. With it he could become what he was born to be. The majesty and grandeur of the silver dragon would be his. He would fly above the clouds. He would spread silver wings beneath the sun. He would finally be free from the dark misery his life had been.

The fire of the dragon's compulsion burned through his mind. With the help of Mudd and the others, he would gain the dragon pendant. But he knew as soon as they found it, he would take it, fighting and killing Mudd, Drakecutter, Iroden, and Hiera if necessary. The thought of it froze his heart. He would gain the life he wanted at the cost of ending theirs.

Hiera moved over to the children, offering them food and water, washing the littlest boy's face. Her golden hair glimmered in the torchlight. She was so beautiful, so compassionate, and so open it made Kirak's heart ache. Mudd stood beside her, reassuring the children that they would find some way to break the enchantment.

Drakecutter stared up at Kirak. "You're the magic-user. Think of something."

Growling, Kirak flung himself across the room and snapped the manacles around his wrists. He would free the children even if it meant spending the rest of eternity chained in this filthy cavern. At least then he would have done one good thing with his life.

As soon as the cold metal closed around his wrists a blue light flashed, blinding him, searing through his flesh and bones.

He fell to his knees, clutching his hands together in pain. Sweat drenched his body.

"Kirak!" Hiera screamed.

The weight of the manacles disappeared from his wrists, and something sharp pressed against the palms of his hands. Hiera's soft fingers brushed his cheek.

Kirak blinked his eyes until they became reaccustomed to the dim cavern. Hiera crouched in front of him. The children's cries and whimpers had ceased. He looked over his shoulder and found them gone, along with the chains and horrible smell that had filled the chamber.

"Are you all right?" Hiera asked.

Kirak swallowed the lump in his throat and stumbled to his feet.

"An illusion," Drakecutter said, thumping his axe handle on the ground in disgust.

Kirak choked. The chains hadn't stopped him from hurting the others. There was nothing left to save them. He hadn't even saved the children, since they had not been real.

Light gleamed from between his fingers. He opened his hands and found a small piece of silver like the one Mudd had retrieved from the ceiling over the chasm.

Mudd stepped forward and lifted it from his palm. "Looks like we passed test number two."

"Kirak did it," Hiera cried. She wrapped her arms around him in a tight hug. Her brown eyes looked at him with love and acceptance.

He touched her golden hair and then pushed her gently away. If she knew who he truly was, she wouldn't look at him like that.

Mudd fingered the two pieces of the silver key while Hiera hovered next to Kirak. Mudd couldn't blame her for liking him. What Kirak had done was brave and noble.

The shards of silver fit together, but would not stay. Another part of the key was still missing. Mudd could picture it in his mind. He put the two pieces in his pocket and cleared his throat. "We should keep going."

"Yes," Kirak said, moving half dazed to a hole in the far wall. The magic might have been only an illusion, but it had not left him unscathed. Even in the dim light, Mudd could see the look of pain in his eyes.

Mudd let him lead, followed by Hiera, then Iroden, and Drakecutter.

The hole led into a smooth, round passage that was carved out rather than a natural part of the cave. The ground was even and free from debris. Mudd's boots tapped against the rocks as he walked along.

The sight of those starving children had not left him untouched either. But what really bothered him was that he had almost lost Kirak. If it hadn't been an illusion, Kirak might have been chained in that horrible cavern forever.

Mudd shuddered. No matter how hard he tried not to care about people, he still did. He knew it was good that the others had come with him, but the thought of them dying left his mouth dry and made his heart pound.

He eased the puzzle out of his pocket and fiddled with it in one hand in the light from his lantern. Drakecutter stopped in his path, and Mudd thumped up against the dwarf in surprise.

Mudd looked up from the puzzle and found everyone standing in front of a stone wall. The passage had reached a dead end.

"Look, it's a mirror," Hiera said. Her high-pitched voice echoed along the passageway. She pointed to a tall silver mirror embedded in the rock.

Kirak eased back to stand beside Mudd. "There are runes above the mirror," he said, holding his lantern high.

"The third test." Mudd slid the puzzle into his pocket. "What does it say, Iroden?"

" 'To go beyond, you must face the truth and embrace it.' " Wonder filled Iroden's voice, and he pushed past Hiera to stand in front of the mirror.

"Mudd, come look at this," Hiera said.

Mudd stepped up beside Hiera. In front of her, Iroden stared into the mirror. His reflection in the glass showed a slender elf dressed in pristine white. A braided gold belt hung at his waist, and the medallion of the Platinum Dragon shimmered at his neck.

His stance was graceful and proud. His long silvery blond hair hung clean and loose. He held a book in his hands, and his eyes were riveted on the pages. His back was half turned to a ragged human family that gestured in supplication.

The woman held a little boy whose arm was twisted at an odd angle, broken most likely. They pleaded for help in silence. All the time Iroden's eyes stayed on the book, unaware of their pleas.

"No," Iroden cried. "That's not me. It was me, but I'm not like that anymore. I would help them. I swear I would, even if they are humans."

He reached out to the mirror as if he could snatch the book out of his reflection's hands. His fingers touched the glass—and sank into it.

Iroden jerked his hand back.

"To go beyond you must embrace the truth," he whispered. "All right. I admit it. I have been blind to people of other races. I see that now, but it doesn't mean that's how I have to be in the future."

He took a deep breath, stepped into the mirror, and vanished.

CHAPTER TWENTY-NINE

Hiera squealed with joy. "I knew he was a Silvanesti. I just knew it."

Mudd chuckled. Ever since Iroden had healed him, Mudd had believed as well. "Who wants to go next?" he asked.

Drakecutter stamped up to the mirror. "I'm not afraid of the truth." He stood there, feet spread in a battle stance, hands clutching his axe.

In the mirror's reflection, Drakecutter looked exactly like himself, standing ready for battle in a field of knee-high cornstalks. He held his father's magic axe. A roar shattered the silence, and a red dragon swooped at him.

The Drakecutter in the mirror dodged the dragon's burning breath and rushed forward, sinking the axe into the dragon's leg. The dragon bellowed and thrashed its tail, leveling the cornstalks. It snapped at Drakecutter, but he dodged and swung the axe into the dragon's slender neck just behind its head.

The magic axe cleaved through the plated scales and neck

frill. The terrible beast sank to the ground, a last plume of smoke lifting from its nostrils.

"I did it!" Drakecutter shouted. His shout reverberated from the walls, reminding Mudd that he was in a dead-end corridor deep underground, not a cornfield.

Drakecutter stepped toward the glass, then hesitated. "The corn," he whispered. The battle with the dragon had churned up the cornfield until not one plant stood. "The entire crop is gone."

"Maybe you could replant it," Hiera said.

Mudd shook his head. "Maybe the mirror is trying to tell you that you can't be both a warrior and a farmer."

"I know what I want to be," Drakecutter growled. He marched forward and disappeared into the glass.

"You were wrong," Hiera said after he'd gone.

"Wrong?" Mudd asked. He wasn't sure he wanted a turn to look into the mirror. He couldn't imagine what he might see.

"Drakecutter isn't a draconian," Hiera said. "If he were, the mirror would have shown us the truth like it did with Iroden."

A shiver went through Mudd. She was right.

"I think I hear something," Kirak said, drawing his swords and looking back the way they'd come. "Maybe it wasn't a good idea to leave the rope strung across the chasm. The gnolls might have come back to the cave and followed us."

Mudd reached for his sword.

"No," Kirak said. "You two go through. I'll watch your back

and come right after. If the gnolls do figure out how to get through the mirror, we can pick them off easily from the other side."

"Right. Go ahead, Hiera," Mudd said, nudging her toward the mirror.

Hiera stepped up to the glass. Her image wavered for a moment, then split in two. On the right stood a ranger dressed in leather armor. She carried a bow slung over her back and Set-ai's dragon claws in her hands.

"Yes," Hiera said, pounding the air with her fist. "I knew he would give them to me someday."

"What about that?" Mudd said, pointing to the second image in the mirror.

The second Hiera's golden hair fell in curls around her shoulders. She wore a lavender dress with a wide ruffle at the bottom. The material swayed and shimmered as she danced gracefully with a faceless young man. Her feminine beauty stood in stark contrast to the cold ranger beside her in the mirror.

Hiera put her hands on her hips. "Well of all the useless. . . ."

Mudd laughed.

"Well, I choose to be a ranger," Hiera said. She stepped into the ranger image—and smashed her face against the glass.

"Maybe not," Mudd said. "See what happens if you go the other way."

"But that's not what I want to be," Hiera said. Her lips drew into a pout.

A rock rattled in the dark passage behind them. "Did you

hear that?" Kirak said. "They're coming. Hurry up and go through the mirror."

"Fine," Hiera said. She rolled her eyes and tried to walk through the beautiful young woman in the glass. Again she accomplished no more than bruising her nose.

"What?" she cried, throwing her hands up in exasperation.

"Try reaching out to both of them," Mudd said. He'd seen glimpses of two sides of his sister and was proud of both.

Hiera placed one hand against the ranger as if taking a dragon claw and the other hand against the dancing young woman. Both hands sank into the mirror, pulling Hiera in after them.

"Your turn," Kirak said. He shuffled and swung his swords in an arc toward their unseen foes.

Mudd stepped up to the mirror.

When he looked into the glass, his own image stared back at him. He had the same messy hair and the same clothes, rumpled and dirty from his journey. His reflection held the same mischievous eyes and smile. He looked exactly like himself, except an empty black spot hung over his chest where his heart would have been.

He touched the blackness, and a lump rose in his throat. He recognized the black hole, though he'd never seen it with his eyes before. The first dark spots had appeared when his parents had died. He'd hidden the emptiness with a wide smile and a laugh.

He had made friends with everyone in an attempt to fill the void. He'd started taking things apart, trying to see how they worked. He constantly sought answers, hoping that if he could just learn how everything went together, he might be able to repair his own heart.

Then Hector had died, and the blackness had blossomed into a gnawing hunger. He was an expert at picking locks and fixing things like the gears of Potter's Mill. But he could not repair himself or banish the emptiness inside.

He never thought the truth would be such a hard test.

"Very well," Mudd said, accepting the ache in his heart. He had to embrace the truth. He had lost people he cared about, and that hurt him. He couldn't go on pretending it didn't, and he couldn't reject everyone else just because he was afraid to lose someone again.

No matter how many locks he picked, the dead would not be waiting for him on the other side of the door. Taking a shaky breath, Mudd stepped forward and moved beyond the dead end that had trapped him.

CHAPTER THIRTY

Kirak slumped against the cold stone and sheathed his swords as soon as Mudd vanished into the mirror. He feared no gnolls. He'd just made that up to convince the others to go first. He'd even thrown the rock off into the darkness to make the sound that hurried them through.

He had no idea why Mudd had thought Drakecutter was a draconian, but he didn't like it. Kirak didn't need to look in the mirror to know what his truth would be. He recognized all too well the monster that lurked inside him.

He knew also what the others' reactions would be. He'd seen the hate and distrust in Mudd's eyes when he looked at Drakecutter. Those murderous glances had been meant for him. He felt betrayed, though he knew he shouldn't. He was the one who would do the betraying.

But it hurt. For a few short days he'd felt like he had friends, people who really cared about him. It was such a small thing to want—and so impossible. He was a loathsome creature. Hated. Feared. Despised.

Kirak shook away the pain and stepped up to the mirror. He wanted to run away instead of looking at himself in the glass, but Redclaw's compulsion wouldn't allow it. He'd started on a path he could not reverse.

The scaly lizard man who stared back at him from the mirror made his stomach churn. Tall heavy body. Thick tail. Sharp claws. And a pair of gray wings that could carry him up into the air, but not far or for long.

He'd been shaped by the magic to be nothing more than a killer. The atrocities he'd committed during the war haunted him.

He touched his face, surprised to feel warm skin beneath his fingers. He'd worn the body of the young squire he'd hewn to bits ever since he'd used it to desert the dragonarmy. But neither the human form nor the draconian were his true self.

"You lie," he whispered to the mirror. "I am a silver dragon, hatched from a silver dragon egg. I don't care what it takes. I will regain my true form."

"Kirak, are you all right?" Mudd's faint voice drifted through the mirror. "I better go back and help him, Hiera."

Growling, Kirak flung himself at the glass before the others could come back through and see the hideous monster that he was.

Mudd heard a growl and dodged just in time to miss being knocked over by Kirak as he came flying through the magical doorway created by the mirror.

Kirak landed on his chest in the soft sand and grunted.

"Kirak?" Hiera tried to touch him, but he jerked away. His face was pale, and his breath came in ragged gasps.

Mudd already had his sword out. He set his stance and waited for a gnoll to come through the mirror after Kirak. Hiera drew back her bow. Drakecutter hefted his axe and growled, ready for battle.

The doorway remained dark and empty.

Kirak shook his head. "They must be too dumb to figure out the mirror. I think we're safe now."

Mudd waited a few more minutes before returning his sword to its sheath. "Good. We just have to find the last part of the key."

The room they stood in was wide, with a ceiling that stretched high overhead. A narrow crack ran in a jagged line along the floor of the cavern from the place they'd entered to a stone doorway on the far side. Familiar runes arched across the top of the doorway. Thick sand covered the floor in lumpy mounds. The smell of decay filled the cavern, though the room was dry compared to the rest of the cave.

Mudd frowned. There was no sign of the third piece of the key. He'd been sure they'd find it once they passed the mirror's test.

"That's strange," Hiera said. "You'd think the key would be here somewhere."

Iroden put his hands in his pocket and shuffled through the sand along with the others. "Hey," he said. "Oh no."

"'Oh no' what?" Mudd asked.

"This is not my fault. I didn't take it," Iroden said, pulling his hand out. Silver light glimmered from his fingers. "I swear I didn't put it in my pocket."

Drakecutter glared at him.

"Of course not, Iroden," Hiera said, patting his shoulder.

Mudd smiled and took the key from Iroden's hand. "I did the first test and found the first piece. Kirak passed the second test and the second piece appeared in his hand. You were the first one through the mirror. It makes sense that you'd get the last piece."

Iroden perked up. "That's right."

Mudd pulled out the other two pieces and snapped the key together. It was a small key, narrow, with delicate scrollwork on the handle. Its blue light warmed his hand. He curled his fist around it and started triumphantly across the chamber.

A pile of sand gave way beneath his feet, twisting his ankle and pitching him forward. He landed face first, the air knocked out of him. A bony hand grabbed his leg.

Sand sprayed up all around the group as skeletal figures burst from their hiding places in the sandy mounds.

Mudd kicked off the hand that held him, jumped to his feet, and came face to face with a hideous monster. Mottled flesh hung across scarred and pitted bones. It might once have been a man, but it looked like a body that had rotted in a grave for years before bursting free. Its red eyes burned with hunger. The stench of decay made Mudd stagger backward, fumbling to unsheath his sword.

The creature lunged at him. Mudd threw his arm up to block, and the silver key spun out of his hands. It arced over his head, pinged against the stone at the rim of the crack that ran along the floor, then toppled inside.

Yelling, Mudd dived after it, but his fingers closed on empty air. The key's light grew fainter and fainter until it vanished into the darkness below.

The monster jumped on his back, gnashing its teeth. Before it had a chance to sink them into Mudd's flesh, Kirak kicked it away. He held two others at bay with his flashing swords.

Mudd lay there, stunned. The key was gone. He looked from the dark crack to the locked stone door across the cavern.

"Get up," Kirak yelled. "They're ghouls. If they claw you, you'll be paralyzed. Go get the door open, quickly."

Mudd jumped to his feet.

Drakecutter swung his axe. It cleaved through one of the ghouls and thunked into the sand. Half of the ghoul's shriveled body fell one way, and the other half fell the other. Two more ghouls raced in to take its place.

Drakecutter cursed and swung again, using the side of his axe to bash one ghoul into the other. The two crashed to the floor but got back up.

"The door!" Kirak called. "Everyone get to the door."

"But the key is gone," Mudd cried as he raced across the chamber. The only escape lay beyond one door or the other, and he refused to go back without the pendant.

Hiera slashed at one of the ghouls and ran to Mudd. "So many of them," she said, panting as she put her back to the door and reset her stance. Her eyes were fixed with steely determination.

Three of the ghouls turned burning eyes on her and advanced, clawing the air with their bony hands.

Drakecutter and Kirak stood back to back, slashing and hacking at the rest of the monsters. Step by step they battled their way toward the door.

"Where's Iroden?" Mudd cried. Then he saw Iroden in the middle of the room where he'd been when the ghouls burst from their hiding places.

Iroden stood frozen in place, one hand clutching his holy medallion, the other outstretched as if to ward off a blow. Blood dripped from a deep scratch in his arm.

"Kirak!" Mudd yelled. "Get Iroden."

A ghoul leaped at Mudd, and he slashed at it with his sword, hitting it across the face. It stumbled back, shook its head, and then came at Mudd again.

Hiera gave up attacking, since her cuts and thrusts didn't seem to even slow the monsters. Instead she used her weapons to block the ghoul's arms as they reached for her. Dull thumps sounded each time their bones made contact with the flat of her blades.

Mudd imitated her, blocking the ghoul's paralyzing claws. His elbow bumped her arm, and she missed a block. Twisting to the side, she dodged the ghoul's outstretched hand.

"Mudd!" she screamed. "Stop flailing around with your sword and pick the lock!"

Right. Mudd sheathed his sword and pulled the lock picks out of his shirt.

While Hiera held the ghouls at bay, Mudd ran his fingers along the rough stone, looking for the keyhole. If there was a key, there had to be a place to stick it in.

Drakecutter reached them, followed by Kirak, who held Iroden under one arm. He propped the paralyzed kender against the wall. Sweat glistened on Kirak's arms and face as he went back to battling the ghouls.

"Hurry!" Kirak yelled at Mudd.

Mudd blinked and stared at the door. He'd felt every inch of it and even inspected the walls beside and above. There was no sign of any keyhole. The door was solid rock.

"Where did all these ghouls come from?" Hiera asked. She sliced off a groping hand and kicked the ghoul in the knee, crunching bone and toppling it backward. Another took its place while the one she felled rose to its feet and shambled forward once again.

"The book said none of the mercenaries made it out of the cave except their leader," Kirak said between slashes with his swords. "Something happened in this chamber. Knowing mercenaries, I'll wager they had a difference of opinion and killed one another off. Or their leader betrayed them, intent on keeping whatever treasure he thought to find for himself."

"You're saying the mercenaries became the ghouls? How?" Hiera asked.

Mudd faced the others to tell them he couldn't find a lock

to pick. Kirak froze at Hiera's questions, and a ghoul leaped at him. It would have sunk its claw into Kirak's chest if Mudd hadn't kicked it in the gut.

It doubled over, then straightened and growled at Mudd, grinding its sharp teeth.

Kirak took a step back from the creature so his body came flat against the stone door. Mudd drew his sword and filled the gap Kirak had left in the protective circle.

"What's wrong? Are you hit?" Mudd asked Kirak.

Kirak shook his head. "No," he said. "The . . . well, sometimes. . . ." His face hardened. "Let's just say that ghouls are created on the death of a living person who savored the taste of human flesh."

"What?" Hiera shrieked.

"It happened sometimes in the dragonarmies during the war," Kirak whispered. His voice barely carried over the clank of steel and crunch of rotting bones. He slammed his fists against the stone door behind him as if he could push it open with sheer strength and escape the monstrosities before him—or whatever memories haunted his mind.

Beneath Kirak's hands, the face of the door changed. What had been unadorned rock shimmered into delicately carved stone with the image of a graceful silver dragon. It was done in such intricate detail that Mudd could make out each individual scale.

"Kirak, look at the door!" Mudd yelled, kicking a ghoul and avoiding a claw that slashed the air in front of his face.

Kirak stepped away and turned around to see the door, but as soon as he stopped touching it, it changed back into unremarkable stone. "Look at what?" he asked. "It's just a door. Why haven't you got it open yet?"

"I couldn't find a keyhole until now," Mudd said. He nodded for Hiera and Drakecutter to take the fight on their own. Then he slid his sword into its sheath and pushed Kirak up against the door.

At Kirak's touch the stone changed back into the carved dragon. And there on the dragon's chest over the heart was a black chink in its scaly armor.

"Stay just like that," Mudd said, snapping up his lock picks and inserting the most likely ones into the hole in the dragon's scales.

"I don't understand," Kirak said.

"Magic," Mudd mumbled while he fiddled with the delicate lock. "You're the wizard. You tell me."

"I don't know. I just have some natural abilities," Kirak protested.

"Well they must be similar to the silver dragon's," Mudd said. "The magic responds to you, and it wouldn't for me." A faint click sounded inside the stone. A grumbling shook the ground, and the rock slid sideways, revealing a chamber beyond.

"Everyone inside," Mudd yelled.

Kirak grabbed Iroden and jumped through the hole. Mudd followed.

"You go next, lass," Drakecutter told Hiera. He chopped off

a ghoul's legs at the knees. It fell to the ground, then came back at him, walking on the stumpy remains of its legs.

Hiera slipped into the room, and Drakecutter backed in after her.

"Touch the entryway," Mudd told Kirak.

Kirak reached out and pressed his hands against the rock beside the open doorway. The rumble returned, and the stone slid over the hole, blocking the ghouls from coming after them.

Kirak had expected darkness. He and Mudd had left their lamps in the chamber beyond, needing both hands to fight the ghouls. But a warm silver light filled the small chamber they'd entered. It came from above a pedestal in the center of the room. A pendant shaped like a silver dragon hung suspended on a chain in the air.

Kirak froze, staring at the pendant as it twisted and glimmered, calling to him from only a few steps away. After years of searching, it was finally his.

Mudd stepped between him and the pendant, reaching for it.

Drakecutter got hold of it first. "I'll summon the dragon," Drakecutter said. "Then we can all tell it what we want."

Iroden groaned and staggered forward, the ghouls' paralysis wearing off. "The pendant!" he cried. "We've found it." His eyes glittered, and he snatched it from Drakecutter's hands. "Let me call the dragon. I can speak to it in its own language. We're more likely to convince it to help more than one person that way."

"Give it to me," Mudd said, towering over Iroden. "I have to save Shemnara."

Kirak tried to back away from the squabbling group, but fire burned through his mind. The dragon's magic tore away his control.

"Mudd, watch out!" he cried.

The moment the words left his mouth, a jagged pain swept through his body. Skin vanished, replaced by scales and heavy armor. His tail thumped the ground, and his flapping wings sent up a spray of sand.

He lunged forward and tore the pendant from Iroden's grip. With a wail of despair, he flung himself to the door they'd come through. He had to get out of there before the others tried to stop him, and he ended up killing them. He clawed the stone, and it opened at his touch.

The pack of ghouls waited just on the other side.

He spread his wings and leaped into the air. He hated to leave the others to fight the ghouls alone, but he knew they had a better chance against the ghouls than against him.

Chapter Thirty-Two

Mudd stared in disbelief as the draconian glided across the chamber, then folded its wings and dived into the black spot on the far wall that led back through the mirror.

The confused pack of ghouls watched the draconian in surprise. As soon as it vanished, they let out feral howls and shambled back toward Mudd and the others.

"Kirak can't be a draconian," Mudd mumbled, drawing his sword. "He willingly sacrificed himself to save those children. A draconian wouldn't do that." Even as Mudd denied it, he felt it was true. Kirak knew things about the dragonarmies that no normal person would.

Hiera blinked back tears and set her stance against the oncoming ghouls. Mudd felt sorry for her. She loved everyone and trusted too easily. He hoped the blow wouldn't destroy her faith in people. But he could see the innocence fading from her eyes. She would not trust so easily again.

The ghouls surged at them through the door.

Drakecutter responded with a war cry and charged the

foul creatures. "Come on," he called to Mudd. "We can't let him get away with the pendant."

That galvanized Mudd into action. He swung his sword at the ghouls. Hiera joined him, hacking and slicing. All fear and revulsion of the undead was lost in the need to go after the draconian.

Iroden stood behind them, clutching his platinum medallion and uttering a prayer to his god. His voice grew strong. He lifted the medallion from around his neck and held it out toward the ghouls.

"In the name of E'li, I rebuke you!" Iroden cried. "Go to your graves, foul creatures. I condemn your souls to the Abyss."

The ghouls wailed and tried to flee. Even as they raced away, their bodies turned to dust and settled to the sandy floor.

Drakecutter's jaw dropped in astonishment. Mudd blinked in surprise. Hiera lifted Iroden from the ground in a big hug.

"Sorry I couldn't do that before," Iroden said after she released him. "I was rather paralyzed."

"Well you're not paralyzed now," Mudd said. "Let's go."

They raced across the chamber and through the mirror. Mudd grabbed his lantern by the doorway. Blood pounded in his ears and he pushed himself to go faster. The initial surprise of Kirak changing into a draconian had worn off, and anger replaced it, along with a fear for Shemnara's life. How could he save her without that pendant?

He could see how the red dragon and the draconian had used him to get the pendant. He doubted that Shemnara had ever meant for him to go after it. They'd just forced her to write the note. But now that they had what they wanted, Shemnara would be of no further use.

The smooth hallway swept past him, and he came to the chamber where the illusionary children had been. Kirak was a magic-user. He must have sensed the illusion and so had no fear that he would really be imprisoned when he put on the chains. He did it only to get the key. A draconian wouldn't care about a few starving children.

Mudd left the cavern behind. A sudden fear shot through him. If Kirak cut the ropes across the chasm, they could be trapped in the cave forever. Mudd slipped through the passage where it grew lower, thankful for his short size. He hoped that the small opening had slowed Kirak enough that they could catch up.

He came out of the passage and stopped with Hiera, Drakecutter, and Iroden pressing around him. Ahead, their rope still spanned the wide black chasm.

Mudd glanced around for any sign of the draconian. The flap of heavy wings overhead startled him. Kirak dropped from above and snatched Iroden up in his claws.

"No!" Hiera screamed as Kirak flew to the chasm.

Kirak hovered for a second, dangling Iroden over the endless drop below. Kirak's silver eyes looked straight into Mudd's. Then he whirled midair, flapped to the far side, and dropped Iroden safely on the ground.

Landing, Kirak raced away up the corridor to the surface.

Mudd stood dumbfounded while Drakecutter and Hiera caught hold of the rope and swung themselves hand over hand across the chasm.

Instead of trapping them there, the draconian had helped Iroden across. Of course, Kirak had traveled with them and knew about Iroden's fear of heights. But Mudd could not fathom why the draconian had helped them once he had the pendant.

"Come on," Hiera called to Mudd.

Mudd rushed forward and crossed the rope to the other side. He left the rope hanging over the chasm and pounded up the passage behind the others.

They reached the narrow entrance just in time to see the draconian glide over the trees and disappear behind the curve of the mountain.

Hiera swore, proving she'd learned more from Set-ai than just how to fight. "Mudd, I'm sorry," she said. "I should have told you."

"Told me what?" Mudd asked. He started down the rocky slope in the direction the draconian had gone.

"I saw Kirak's footprints in the sand back there in the cave," Hiera said. "They looked just like the ones we saw in the field by the dragon tracks. But I couldn't believe it. I thought I must have been remembering wrong." She brushed her hand across her eyes.

"He fooled us all," Drakecutter said. "Don't go blaming yourself."

Mudd agreed. "It's not your fault, Hiera. It's the draconian's.

Those stubby wings can't carry him far. Can you track him?"

Hiera nodded.

"Hold on just a moment," Iroden said, dropping to his knees. He clutched his medallion and whispered a prayer to E'li. The jagged claw marks on his arm stopped bleeding and knit together.

"I'm glad you're with us," Mudd said.

Iroden smiled. "I'm glad I came too."

"Let's go," Hiera urged. "When we get the pendant, maybe we can ask the silver dragon to change Iroden back into an elf. But if we don't hurry, we might be too late. Whatever the draconian and red dragon intend to do with it, it can't be good."

Mudd gritted his teeth in determination. For Shemnara's sake, he had to get the pendant back. For Iroden's sake as well, and Drakecutter's. He wouldn't let his friends down, even if it meant chasing the draconian all the way across the Vingaard Mountains.

CHAPTER THIRTY-THREE

Kirak clutched the pendant in his scaly claw as he raced up the mountainside. He flapped his wings, giving length and speed to his strides. He'd been in human form so long he'd forgotten how much faster he could move as a draconian.

His heart pounded with excitement. He'd done it, managed to get the pendant without killing any of his friends. Did he dare call them friends? They wouldn't think of him as a friend anymore.

That dark thought was doused by the new hope that kindled inside him.

Redclaw had been right. Her plan was the only way. He would summon the silver dragon and kill it, allowing him to change into the dragon's form. Then he would become what he was always meant to be. As soon as he turned into a silver dragon, he'd take care of Redclaw. She hadn't thought of that. Kirak would become as large and powerful as she was. No more would her compulsion force him to do things he didn't like.

Trees raced past him and he panted, pushing himself

hard to go up the final slope to Redclaw's cave.

Redclaw waited for him inside. The heat of her breath sent ripples rising over her horde. In her claw a fist-sized ruby pulsed with red light.

Kirak skidded to a stop, toppling a pile of steel coins. The sharp claws on his feet clicked against the stone as he used his tail to steady himself.

"It's about time," Redclaw said. "Did you bring me the pendant?"

Kirak opened his fist and showed her the graceful silver dragon in his hand.

"Very well," she said. She wormed her way to a lump of black rock she'd set up at the side of the cave. The pulsing ruby fit into an iron claw protruding from the top of the rock. "You may summon the silver dragon now." She laughed deep in her throat. "Sleekwing Thunderbolt, your time is finished."

"Just a minute," Kirak said. He shoved the pendant under his armor and raced across the cave to the alcove where he'd left Shemnara.

She lay limp and pale on the bed he'd made for her. One side of her dress was blackened and her arm blistered and burned. The food and water he'd left for her were gone. He'd taken too long to return.

"Shemnara?" He knelt beside her, listening for a breath or a heartbeat.

Her eyes fluttered open, and she looked up at him.

"You're alive. Good." He got his pack off his back. His

wings made carrying it uncomfortable, but he'd refused to leave it behind. He pressed his water skin to her lips and urged her to drink.

Coins clinked and treasure banged as Redclaw crawled across the cave toward him, grumbling beneath her hot breath.

Kirak unlocked the chain that bound Shemnara and arranged it so it looked like it still held her.

Redclaw stuck her head into the alcove. "What are you doing, you miserable worm?" she bellowed.

Kirak whipped around to face her, his tail thunking against the wall. He'd need to get used to having it again. "Nothing. Just checking on the old woman."

"She's of no further use to us," Redclaw growled.

Kirak dropped his gaze to his feet and refused to meet Redclaw's eyes.

"Kill her, and lets get on with this," the dragon commanded.

"Whatever you say." Kirak pulled out his swords.

Redclaw lumbered back into the main cavern to her position beside the ruby.

Kirak lifted his swords and swung them one after another into his pack. The blades thumped and sliced through the leather.

Shemnara—Paladine bless her—let out a ragged cry and then fell silent.

She winked at him. He nodded to her, sheathed his swords, and stepped out into the cavern. He strode through the mass of treasure to where he'd thrown Drakecutter's axe.

Picking it up, he felt the magic pulse in his hands.

"Fool," Redclaw hissed. "Don't let Sleekwing see that until it's time."

Out of the corner of his eye, Kirak saw Shemnara creep from her prison. He swung the axe, imagining what it would feel like to cut through dragon scales, to see an invincible dragon fall.

"What if I've changed my mind?" Kirak cried, trying to keep Redclaw's attention on himself. "I might be happy as a red dragon instead of a silver."

Redclaw hissed and lunged to the cave entrance, wrapping her claws around the fleeing Shemnara.

"Kirak, Kirak," Redclaw said in a deep growl. "I suppose the old woman is still useful after all. Put that axe down and summon the silver dragon now, or I'll tear Shemnara's guts out and eat her one limb at a time while she dies slowly and painfully."

Kirak dropped the axe. Always Redclaw outwitted him. He'd only wanted to provide a distraction so Shemnara could get away.

Redclaw carried Shemnara to the ruby and blew a warning lick of flame at Kirak.

Kirak pulled out the dragon pendant and held it in his palm with the chain looped around his hand. Carved in delicate script down the dragon's back was the silver dragon's true name.

Kirak lifted the pendant so it sparkled in the thin stream of light from the cave's entrance. "Niterealatus Fulminis!" he shouted.

A pulse of magic cracked from the pendant and sped out of the cave across the sky like a wide finger of lightning. The cave fell silent, waiting.

"When she comes," Redclaw hissed, "keep her attention fixed on you and draw her to the back of the chamber."

Outside a dark cloud moved in front of the sun. The temperature dropped, and thick mist filled the entryway.

Kirak tensed. His moment had come.

Great wings beat the air outside. A sleek form that looked like it had been forged from molten silver landed in the entrance and ducked into the cave. The silver dragon's mercury-colored eyes fell on the pendant Kirak clutched in his hand. She stepped forward, and her gaze locked on him.

Kirak stumbled back to the rear of the cave, trying to break eye contact. He couldn't look such a glorious being in the face.

"You have summoned me, little dragon?" The silver dragon's voice sounded like the song of the wind dancing across the sky.

Kirak dropped to his knees in the face of the dragon's majesty. That's what he should have been, not a stunted, loathsome draconian.

"You have called, and I have come," the silver dragon continued, leaning over him. "What is it you wish?"

Redclaw's voice rumbled an incantation from the shadows. A net of red light shot from the ruby and enveloped Sleekwing.

Sleekwing roared and tried to break free, but the net held her frozen, a silver statue, majestic and immobile.

Redclaw slithered out to face her enemy. She still held Shemnara. "Get the axe," she commanded Kirak.

Kirak hesitated.

Redclaw pressed her claw into Shemnara's side, and Shemnara cried out in pain. Swearing, Kirak dropped the pendant and raced across the room to the fallen axe.

CHAPTER THIRTY-FOUR

Redclaw stopped in front of Sleekwing. "I knew you were searching the mountains for something precious. How ironic that I found it first. I am going to enjoy watching it destroy you. I told you I'd get revenge."

Kirak picked up the axe with shaking hands and strode to the imprisoned dragon. One swift stroke, and he would become a silver dragon in Sleekwing's place.

"Kirak, don't!" Shemnara cried.

Redclaw shook her, and she fell silent.

"It's the only way," Kirak said. "Perhaps if you would have told me where the Dragon Well was I could have dipped myself into it, and it would have transformed me into my rightful shape. But you sent me after the pendant instead. Now I have to finish the quest that you started."

"Killing isn't the answer," Shemnara said.

"Of course it is," Redclaw roared. "Especially if you want me to spare the old woman's life."

Kirak bowed his head and stepped up to the silver dragon.

Her massive body towered above him, but her neck was within his reach since she'd been leaning over him when Redclaw trapped her. Misty light from outside illuminated the dragon's shiny scales. She smelled like blue sky after a rainstorm.

The axe rested heavily in his hands. It was time to kill once more, but never again after. He lifted the axe high over his head and stepped into the swing.

"I think he's in *there.*" Kirak's sensitive ears picked up Hiera's voice outside the cave.

Kirak froze and glanced from the silver dragon to the entryway. He saw no sign of Hiera and the others but could hear the scrabble of rocks and dirt outside.

"Don't come in here!" he yelled. Fools. They'd followed him.

Mudd, Hiera, and Drakecutter leaped into the cave, their weapons drawn and ready. Hiera had an arrow on her bowstring. Mudd held his sword and dagger. Drakecutter hefted his battle-axe. Iroden peered around the entrance, his medallion clutched in his hand.

Kirak stiffened, gripping the axe he held poised over the silver dragon's neck.

"What are you doing?" Hiera shrieked. "Kirak, put down the axe or I'll shoot you. I swear I will." She pointed her arrow at Kirak and pulled back the string.

Redclaw let loose a playful rumble, dropped Shemnara, and advanced on the intruders.

Hiera shifted her aim and shot at the advancing red

dragon. Her arrow pinged off Redclaw's scales. Iroden yelped. Kirak figured the kender probably would have run if he hadn't been overcome with dragonfear.

"So Kirak was working with you," Mudd said to Redclaw. He stood his ground. Hate burned in his eyes. "You planned this whole thing."

"Yes, I did," Redclaw said. "Kirak couldn't get the pendant on his own."

Redclaw's words stung Kirak, and he lowered the axe.

"Of what use is the pendant to you?" Drakecutter growled at Redclaw. He edged away from Mudd, as if he could pin a dragon a hundred times larger than himself between them.

Kirak shook his head. They'd followed him straight into the dragon's clutches.

Hiera set a second arrow on the string and aimed at Redclaw's eye.

Redclaw batted her into the wall before her fingers had time to let go. Hiera crunched against the stone and slid to the ground.

Kirak's heart leaped into his throat, and he stepped toward her.

Drakecutter howled in outrage. He raced forward, swinging his axe. Redclaw stood still and let him hit her. The axe and handle shattered in Drakecutter's hands.

Redclaw snorted with laughter.

Mudd's eyes met Kirak's and went to the axe in his hands. Understanding registered on Mudd's face. Kirak could tell Mudd knew he'd intended to kill the silver dragon and why. Kirak's face grew hot with shame. Mudd's eyes traced the lines of the glowing red net that held Sleekwing in place. His gaze followed the light back to its origin in the ruby at the side of the cave.

The dragon swiped at Mudd.

Mudd flipped over the dragon's claw and landed on his feet. Instead of striking the dragon with his sword, he sheathed his weapon, dodged beneath the dragon's torso, and leaped up on Redclaw's treasure horde.

"So much for the fierce red dragon," Mudd shouted. "You can't even fight your own battles. Can't even kill your own enemies. So pathetic. You have to beg a useless draconian to do the job."

Kirak shuddered.

Mudd's taunt angered Redclaw, and she turned away from Drakecutter, Iroden, and Hiera. She sucked in a breath, stoking the fire in her belly.

Mudd snatched up a silver scepter and a shimmering diamond necklace. "Go ahead," he cried.

Redclaw roared in frustration and released the cone of fire at the solid rock above. She had no desire to melt her hoard into a pile of useless slag.

Kirak laughed at Mudd's ability to outwit her.

Redclaw's gaze fell on Kirak. Her molten eyes locked with his. Fear of what she would make him do shot through him, but he couldn't tear his gaze away.

"Kill the silver dragon," Redclaw hissed.

Fire burned through Kirak's mind. *Kill the silver dragon. Kill the silver dragon.* The command resonated inside him.

He heard another arrow ping off Redclaw's scales. Hiera screamed. Swords clanked and treasure rattled.

Kirak lifted the axe over his head. One strike. That's all it would take, and he would become a silver dragon. But for some reason his free will set its stance in the middle of his mind and fought the dragon's fiery compulsion.

Your friends are dying, it screamed at him.

He gripped the axe handle so hard it would have broken if it hadn't been magic. *If I become a silver dragon, I can help them,* he argued with himself.

But would a silver dragon murder a helpless creature? his mind retorted. If you swing that axe it will be murder. Even if you do take the silver dragon's form, you'll be nothing more than the loathsome draconian you've always been—a killer. Evil. Wretched.

The fire wrapped around his free will in a ball of burning pain, but he fought his way through it.

"Drakecutter!" Kirak screamed and hurled the axe to the dwarf, who had found a two-handed sword in the treasure pile and was striking at Redclaw's leg.

Drakecutter dropped the sword and snatched the axe out of the air.

Kirak launched himself at Redclaw, landing on her back and clawing at the steely red scales.

CHAPTER THIRTY-FIVE

Mudd tumbled down the side of the horde and watched as Drakecutter snatched the magic axe from the air and planted it in the dragon's leg.

The dragon roared in pain. Her fiery breath heated the cavern, making sweat stream down Mudd's face and back.

The draconian leaped onto the dragon, biting and tearing. Though Kirak's claws and teeth couldn't penetrate past the dragon scales, he split the dragon's attention between himself and Drakecutter.

Mudd darted around the dragon to where Hiera lay bleeding. Her second arrow had come within a hairsbreadth of the dragon's eye and angered it into clawing her to the ground.

Iroden crouched next to her, pleading with his god.

Mudd opened Hiera's pack and tore through the contents. His hand closed around her red box. He jerked it free and raced to the side of the cave.

The dragon roared again as Drakecutter hit her with his father's axe. She got her claws around him, tore him and his axe free from her leg, and flung him away.

Bellowing, she clawed at the draconian on her back.

Mudd flipped Hiera's box open, letting the comb clatter to the floor. Drakecutter had grand ideas about killing dragons, but Mudd figured he needed a little help.

The ruby sat on the rock in front of Mudd. Lines of red light shot out from the facets, forming the net around the silver dragon. "And mirrors reflect light," Mudd whispered. He rearranged the squares of Hiera's mirror, then reached up and set them over the side of the glimmering ruby.

He felt the shock of magic as the red light hit the mirrors in his hand. For a moment he thought it would burst through and consume him, but the mirrors worked, diverting the light from around the silver dragon and casting the net onto the red.

"Just like repositioning the gears on Potter's Mill," Mudd crowed. The net wavered as Mudd moved his hand in his exuberance.

"Drakecutter, finish it," he called.

Drakecutter scrambled to his feet.

The red dragon bellowed at being held frozen in her own trap. The sound of her roar shook the cavern. She strained against the fiery red net, muscles bulging, but it held her immobile.

"Hurry," Mudd said. His hand tingled from the magic coursing through the mirror.

The silver dragon grabbed the fallen pendant and slid to the front of the cave, out of range of the net, in case Mudd lost control.

Drakecutter marched across the room and surveyed the red dragon, deciding where best to hit her. She already bled from a couple of places on her legs, but those wounds weren't serious enough to stop her if the magical restraint failed.

The draconian on the dragon's back hunched frozen in place beneath the net. "In the neck below the neck frill, just like you saw in the mirror," he called.

Drakecutter looked up at the towering dragon. She'd reared up, her head turned to the side to get the draconian off her back.

Mudd's hand wavered, and the net slipped.

The dragon roared and came back down on all fours. She sucked in, ready to breathe a cone of fire that would destroy Drakecutter and the axe.

Kirak leaped from the dragon's back and dived for Drakecutter. He caught the dwarf up in his claws and lifted him into the air, just as the fire belched forth, turning a chest of steel coins into molten slag.

The dragon screamed in fury.

Mudd fought to get the magic net back under control. Steadying his hand, he reset the mirrors. The net reformed over the red dragon, but Mudd knew he couldn't hold it for long. He was meddling with powerful magic that could vaporize him with one slip of the hand.

Flapping furiously, Kirak flew Drakecutter through the air and hovered within range of the dragon's neck. Drakecutter swung his axe. It crunched through thick scales, severing the monstrous head, killing the red dragon.

Gasping in relief, Mudd dived away from the pulsing ruby. Hiera's mirror clattered to the cave floor. The red lines of the net shimmered for a moment, then faded, their power doused by the dragon's death.

Mudd raced to Shemnara. She lay on the ground where the dragon had dropped her, her face pale, her right arm burned. He drew her onto his lap, cradling her head in his hands.

Her wrinkled fingers patted his arm. "You've done well, my boy," she said. Then her eyes closed and she fell unconscious.

"Iroden!" Mudd yelled.

Iroden appeared around the side of the red dragon's corpse and stumbled through the scattered treasure toward Mudd. He looked exhausted from healing Hiera, but he hurried over.

"Is this Shemnara?" he whispered. "I guess you don't need to ask the silver dragon to get her back."

Mudd smiled at his little friend. "No, not anymore. But can you heal her?"

"Yes, E'li willing." Iroden clutched his medallion and began to pray.

Kirak set Drakecutter on his feet near the dragon's severed head. Then he folded his wings and settled to the ground. The two looked at each other for a moment, and then Drakecutter backed away, hefting his axe just in case Kirak decided to attack.

Kirak shook his head and strode to the cave's entrance, his tail lashing back and forth.

Mudd's gut ached. He'd heard so many horrible stories about bloodthirsty draconians. They were like devils sprung from the

Abyss itself, delighting in torture and murder.

But somehow Kirak was different. He could have killed them all back in the cave where they'd found the pendant, but he hadn't. He could have cut the ropes and left them trapped. Instead he made sure Iroden crossed safely. Then he fought against his own red dragon.

Mudd eased Shemnara to the ground, patted Iroden's shoulder, and went after the retreating draconian.

He found Kirak standing in the cave's entrance, face to face with the silver dragon.

Mudd had been around dragons enough to know dragonfear when he felt it, but what washed over him was not fear. It was a bone-deep reverence and adoration, and it held him immobile while the draconian and dragon spoke.

"You did the right thing, little dragon," the silver said.

Kirak glanced at the red dragon and shuddered. "I don't like killing."

"No silver dragon does." The dragon lowered her head to look Kirak in the eyes. "You have yet to ask me for a boon. What is your wish, little one?"

Kirak glanced at Drakecutter, who held his father's axe. Then he looked from Mudd to Iroden, who still knelt beside Shemnara, clutching his medallion with his head bowed in prayer. Mudd wondered what Kirak would wish for.

Kirak pointed at Iroden. "The . . . the kender is really a Silvanesti elf," he said. "Please, can you turn him back to his true form?"

The silver dragon let out a low rumbling laugh. "Of course I can. The image of the kender is only an illusion." She waved her claw toward Iroden and spoke a string of words in the language of magic.

Iroden shimmered. Then the kender vanished, replaced by a graceful elf. Iroden leaped to his feet. His hands smoothed his flowing white robes and straightened the golden belt at his waist. He stared in wonder at the silver dragon and the draconian.

Mudd stepped forward and clasped Kirak's thick arm. "Thank you," he said.

Kirak shied away. A look of pain and sorrow filled his eyes, and he turned his head.

CHAPTER THIRTY-SIX

irak," the silver dragon's voice had changed into a soft feminine tone.

Kirak snapped his gaze back to the dragon. Sleekwing was gone. In her place stood Nitere, the beautiful silver-haired Aesthetic they'd met at the library in Palanthas. Tears glistened in her eyes. Her right arm had healed since they'd left her.

Kirak gripped his sword hilts and shuffled his feet, whipping his tail back and forth. He should have known Nitere was a dragon from the way she'd delved into his mind, forcing him to relive those horrible memories.

"My baby. My dear child." Nitere wrapped her arms around him and stroked his back with her soft hands. "You are not the devil you think you are. I saw your memories. You defeated the abishai that would have possessed you. Your body is warped, but your heart is true. You are a silver dragon as much as I am."

She pulled away. "Do you think that because I now look like a human woman that I am no longer a silver dragon?"

It took Kirak a moment to remember to speak. Her words

had stunned him. She'd called him her child. Could it be true? And she'd hugged him, something that only Hiera had done before—and not while he was in draconian form.

"Hiera?" Kirak turned back to the cave. Last he'd seen her, she'd been hurt, dying. He found her standing close by, healed by Iroden, rubbing at her eyes. Iroden and Drakecutter came up beside her.

"Is he really your son?" Hiera asked. "How can you tell?"

"A mother knows her child," Nitere said. "Losing our eggs was the most devastating thing for us dragons. We would have done anything to ensure their safety. Unfortunately we did the wrong thing, believing the evil dragons when they told us they'd not harm our eggs if we stayed out of the war. We found out the Dark Queen's real plans too late to save the hatchlings. They had all been changed to draconians."

Hiera gasped and rested sad eyes on Kirak. Kirak looked away, unable to bear her pity.

"I had given up all hope," Nitere said, "until I felt Kirak's presence during the war. I've been looking for him ever since. The other silver dragons called it folly. No draconian could have the heart of a silver dragon. So I created the pendant and the tests. Kirak passed them. Now no one can dispute that he is my son." She lifted the dragon pendant in her hand and set it gently around Kirak's neck.

Kirak touched the warm metal and looked into the silver eyes of the woman who claimed to be his mother. "But . . . I didn't pass all the tests. Mudd and the others helped."

"Yes, your friends." Nitere gazed warmly at Mudd, Hiera, Drakecutter, and Iroden. "I think you will always find that you can accomplish more in the company of friends than by yourself."

Her eyes lingered on Mudd for a long moment.

Mudd flushed, and his hand went to his pocket, drawing out the puzzle he often played with.

Kirak stared down at his scaly, clawed feet and spoke to Nitere. "You have great powers. If you truly believe I am your son, will you change me into the dragon I should have been?"

Nitere sighed. "I wish I could. If only it were as simple as lifting an illusion like Iroden's. The evil magic split your body into several parts, creating more than one draconian. I don't know where the other hatchlings are from your egg, and we could not reclaim them if I did. They are no more than receptacles for the abishai that possess them. You are only a small part of the whole. I can't change you into something bigger than you are."

Kirak's heart sank. "Then killing you or some other silver dragon is the only way." He realized he could never do such a thing.

Nitere snorted, a noise that sounded much more dragon than human. "Is that what Redclaw told you?" She shook her head disdainfully at the fallen red dragon. "It wouldn't have worked. You can only take the shape of something your own size or smaller."

A shiver ran down Kirak's spine. Redclaw had lied to him.

If he had killed Sleekwing, he would have destroyed his own mother and gotten nothing in return.

"I refuse to kill anymore," Kirak said bitterly. "I'll be stuck as a draconian forever."

"Only if you want to be." Nitere smiled and laid a gentle hand on his shoulder.

"What do you mean?" Kirak asked.

"I can't change you into something bigger than you are, but I have instilled much of my own power into the pendant. As long as you wear it, you can change form as you like between human and draconian. And, of course, you can use it to call me anytime. I know you long to fly above the clouds. I can take you there."

A ripple of joy passed through Kirak, and he hugged Nitere to him, careful not to smash her delicate body against his thick armored hide.

"Now, little dragon," Nitere whispered in his ear. "All dragons must have a true name. As your mother, I get the honor of giving it to you. I name you Argentum Veruscordis, which means Sterling Trueheart in Common. Hold that name safe, for it has great power."

Nitere smiled and patted his cheek, then turned her attention to the others. "You should get Shemnara home as soon as possible. She is an old woman, and this damp cave is not good for her."

"It's so far. Shemnara isn't strong enough," Mudd said, frowning.

"She will return to your village the same way she came here," Nitere said. "I am big enough to carry all of you."

She shifted back into her dragon form, Sleekwing Thunderbolt, the magnificent silver dragon. "Come, Sterling. Get Shemnara and climb on my back."

Kirak stood puzzled for a moment, unused to the sound of his new name. Sterling. The name settled over him and felt comfortable. He strode over to Shemnara and lifted her in his strong draconian arms.

The others gathered around him.

He looked into their faces, fearing the revulsion he would see in their eyes. He had hidden his true identity from them, betrayed them, and taken the dragon pendant. Despite what Nitere said about him having the heart of a silver dragon, they had reason to distrust and hate him.

"I'm sorry," Sterling stammered. "I was under the dragon's compulsion. I tried to warn you. I tried to walk away so many times."

"But you didn't walk away," Iroden said, smoothing his robes. "You didn't abandon us. You knew I couldn't cross the chasm on my own, and you stayed to help."

Iroden rested a graceful hand on Sterling's arm. "I have learned a hard lesson during my time as a kender. E'li cares only for what is in our hearts. I am proud to say that I am your friend."

Hiera squealed and hugged Iroden, and then Sterling and Drakecutter.

Drakecutter cleared his throat and stepped away, his face flushed. "I judged you wrong, Sterling. Thanks for helping me kill the dragon."

"You're welcome," Sterling said. "I guess it's time to leave." He nodded toward Sleekwing.

"Go ahead," Mudd said, motioning them to the mouth of the cave. "I'll be right there."

Sterling carried Shemnara out and climbed onto Sleekwing's back. Hiera and Drakecutter swung up behind him.

Iroden hesitated. "I don't think I'm really up to flying."

Drakecutter let out a deep laugh. "You want to go back down that cliff we climbed this morning on your own?"

Iroden's face went pale.

"Don't worry," Sleekwing said. "I promise I won't let you fall."

Mudd joined them, carrying a heavy chest under each arm.

Sterling shifted back to give Mudd room to climb onto Sleekwing in front of him. From the rattle and clank inside the chests, he figured Mudd had helped himself to some of Redclaw's hoard.

Hiera rolled her eyes. "What do you think you're doing?"

An enormous grin spread across Mudd's face. "It sure would be a shame to waste all this treasure, especially with two villages needing to be rebuilt. This should be enough to do it, though I think I might come back here someday to get the rest."

Sleekwing snorted and launched herself into the sky. Cool

air slid past Sterling's face. Exhilaration filled him as they rose higher and higher. Cottony clouds billowed around him. The wind sang across the sky, and his heart sang with it.

CHAPTER THIRTY~SEVEN

Mudd's stomach flip-flopped as Sleekwing dived toward Palanthas. The smell of warm rain clung to the speeding air that blew in his face, making his eyes water.

He clung to the treasure chests to keep them from flying off. The thick wood pressed into his arms, but Mudd wouldn't have given up the chance to fly on Sleekwing for anything. He whooped as she pulled up sharply and settled to the ground on the open lawn in front of the glistening Temple of Paladine.

Iroden stood shaking, his face white. "You sure you don't need me to come to Greenhollow and heal your father?" he asked Drakecutter.

Drakecutter shook his head, sending his braided beard flapping this way and that. "We have a cleric of Mishakal. My father should be fine now that I've recovered his axe."

"All right." Iroden shook Drakecutter's hand, then wrapped an arm around Hiera and hugged her before she could do the same to him.

"Good-bye, Hiera," he said. "I'm not going to forget you.

You were the first person in all of Krynn who showed any kindness to me."

Mudd smiled at the tears glistening in Hiera's eyes.

"You *better* not forget me," Hiera said. "Since you're such a good scribe, I expect letters from you often."

Iroden laughed. "I'll do that." He nodded to Sterling and wished him luck with his new life.

Mudd freed a hand from his treasure to shake Iroden's. "Thanks for your help. We couldn't have succeeded without you. Are you headed home now, or will you stay here at the temple?"

Iroden frowned. "I think I need to stay here for a bit and take care of some things."

Mudd grinned.

Iroden slid down from Sleekwing's back, waved good-bye, and strode up the steps into the temple. Acolytes and clerics bowed and ushered him inside, showing proper respect for the noble elf.

"Those stupid clerics," Hiera muttered. "They'll accept him now that he's an elf, but they wouldn't when he was a kender."

Mudd smiled. "Something tells me that a certain servant of Paladine is about to straighten them out."

"Hold tight," Sleekwing said as she lifted back into the air. "We have a long flight ahead of us."

It *was* a long flight, and Mudd's legs were chafed raw by the time she settled on the ground near the burned dwarf village.

Sleekwing hunched down for Drakecutter to dismount.

Drakecutter stared at his father's dry, empty fields and shook his head. "No one's been watering the poor seeds."

True, the dwarves seemed more intent on reconstructing their homes. An old dwarf with short gray stubble on his chin limped out to them. As he drew closer, Mudd realized it was Stonefist.

Mudd thought Drakecutter's father looked pretty good for someone whose beard had been burned clear off and body blistered by the fire. The dwarf cleric must have been able to heal him as soon as Drakecutter got the axe.

"Father!" Drakecutter cried with delight. He leaped from the dragon's back and raced over to meet him. "I got it," he said, shaking the axe. "And I killed the red dragon."

Stonefist smiled and slapped his son on the back. "I guess I was wrong. You are a warrior, not a farmer." A trace of disappointment touched his voice.

"Yes, I am a warrior," Drakecutter said. His eyes strayed to the field. "And I don't think we should let the cornfield dry out like that just because you've been too hurt to care for it." He shoved the axe into his father's hands, waved to Mudd and the others, and stomped off to the field.

Stonefist hefted the axe, nodded to Mudd, and limped back toward his house.

"Wait," Mudd called. He slid off Sleekwing's back and hurried after the old dwarf, carrying one of the chests of steel.

Stonefist grunted as Mudd came up beside him. "I

thought I told you to keep Greenthumb from going after the red dragon."

Mudd laughed. "Things didn't work out exactly like I planned. But I brought you this." He set the heavy chest on Stonefist's porch. "It's for the whole village. To help rebuild."

Stonefist lifted the lid and stared in wonder at the chest full of steel. "I guess I can forgive you for risking my son's life," he grumbled.

Mudd bowed to the old dwarf and returned to Sleekwing. They had one more flight to make, and Mudd was anxious to get to the end of it.

Sleekwing lifted them with powerful strokes over the mountain peaks. Then she dived down in a graceful glide, skimming the treetops until Potter's Mill came into view. Rebuilding had progressed slower at Mudd's village than it had at Drakecutter's.

The mill was still in ruins, with the blackened skeleton of the waterwheel hanging listlessly in the river. Much of the town looked abandoned, as if the people just didn't have the heart left to rebuild. Mudd figured that would change when people saw Shemnara and the chest of steel Mudd had brought back with her.

Sleekwing landed in the street next to Shemnara's house. Mudd jumped off and reached up to take Shemnara from Sterling.

Sterling climbed down instead, keeping Shemnara safe in his strong grip. He'd carried her the entire way, refusing to allow Shemnara the pain of sitting on the hard dragon scales. Shemnara had slept most of the time, only waking for a few moments now and again.

"Set-ai," Hiera called, sliding off the dragon beside Mudd.

Set-ai stepped out of the house onto the wide porch. He whooped in excitement at seeing them and raced into the street. Hiera wrapped him in a big hug, which he returned until he saw Sterling holding Shemnara. His remaining hand went to his side, looking for a weapon.

"No." Mudd grabbed Set-ai's arm. "Sterling is our friend."

Set-ai swore and pulled away. "What kind of name is that for a draconian? You realize he's probably the one that took Shemnara in the first place. I'll bet he's working with the red dragon."

"And you'd be right," Mudd said, "and wrong at the same time. Sterling helped us destroy the red dragon."

Sleekwing lowered her massive head to glare at Set-ai. "Sterling is my son," she hissed.

Set-ai took a step backward. He held his hand up in a placating gesture. "All right. Who am I to argue with a silver dragon? But folks around here don't like draconians. You better take him with you when you go."

Sterling's eyes fell, and he held Shemnara out to Mudd.

"Take her inside," Mudd said, gesturing to the house. "You're staying right here in Potter's Mill with Hiera and me."

"But he can't," Set-ai said. "He's a draconian. He'll be killed."

Hiera glared at Set-ai and whispered something in Sterling's ear.

Sterling smiled and freed a hand to rub across the silver dragon pendant that hung from his neck. He changed form in front of their eyes, suddenly becoming a lanky youth with long dark hair.

Set-ai stared at Sterling in wonder. "But you can't do that unless you kill someone."

"A silver dragon can change form whenever he wishes," Sterling answered.

Mudd and Hiera both laughed. They all started into the house, but Sleekwing called Mudd back to her.

Mudd left the chest on the porch, stepped up to the dragon, and bowed. "Thanks for your help."

Sleekwing returned his bow. "And thank you for yours. Few humans would embrace friendship with a draconian."

Mudd clutched the gnome's puzzle in his pocket. Just because he'd lost one good friend, didn't mean he couldn't become friends with someone else.

"I think I know someone who can help you solve that puzzle," Sleekwing said.

Mudd jumped in surprise.

Sleekwing gave him a wide, dragonish smile. "In the Hidden City of K'Aal, I've heard there is a gnome who is very good at handling mechanical devices. When he creates things, it seems they actually work." She laughed. "I've heard he's even made a repeating crossbow, of all things."

A rush of excitement went through Mudd. "Hector?" The repeating crossbow had been Hector's invention. But Hector couldn't be in some strange hidden city. He'd died in the fire at Viranesh Keep. Still, what if he somehow survived?

"Where is this hidden city?" Mudd asked.

The dragon shrugged. "If you go to the town of Purespring, perhaps a young woman by the name of Catriona Goodlund can lead you to it."

"What?" Hiera's shrill voice filled the air. She raced down the steps and skidded to a halt next to Mudd.

Sterling followed her out of the house.

"What's she talking about, Mudd?" Hiera babbled.

"A new quest," Mudd said, fingering his puzzle. "One I intend to take as soon as Shemnara is well enough for me to leave her."

"You're not going without me," Hiera said.

"Or me," Sterling added. He rested his hands on his sword hilts.

"Of course not," Mudd said.

The silver dragon nodded her majestic head and leaped into the sky.

Mudd put his arms around Hiera and Sterling and walked with his friends back into Shemnara's house.

R.D. HENHAM is a scribe in the great library of Palanthas. In the course of transcribing stories of legendary dragons, the author felt a gap existed in the story of the everydragon: ordinary dragons who end up doing extraordinary things. With the help of Sindri Suncatcher and fellow scribes, R.D. has filled that gap with these books.

REBECCA SHELLEY has a great love for magical things, especially dragons and fairies. Her four children are her biggest fans. She lives with them and her husband in Salt Lake City, Utah, where they often go on exciting adventures in the rugged Wasatch Mountains. She has written a number of books and stories for children and adults; *Red Dragon Codex* is her first novel published by Mirrorstone.

ACKNOWLEDGEMENTS

I'd like to thank the great cast of people who have taught me and helped me with my writing along the way. This book would not have been possible without those named here and many others.

First I have to thank Honorable Scribe Henham, who asked my assistance on this project. And then I'd like to thank Mrs. Brown, my ninth grade teacher at Union Jr. High, who was the first person to really encourage me in my writing.

Special thanks to Ken Rand who took me under his wing and taught me how to edit my own work, to Jeanne Cavelos who put together and teaches the Odyssey workshop, and to all the Odyssey alumni for their support.

I can't begin to express my thanks to Kris Rusch and Dean Smith for their teaching and encouragement, and to the Oregon Writers Network.

Special thanks to Jonathan for helping me brainstorm, to my daughter Kimberly for giving a child's perspective, and to my husband Dave and the gaming group—Charlie, Carl, Magen, and Anthony—for providing the resources and knowledge of the Dragonlance world.

Above all thanks to my editor, Stacy Whitman, for giving me the opportunity to write about my favorite character and play in this world for a while.

Rebecca Shelley
Assistant to R.D. Henham

There are still nine more dragons to discover!

Join Tatelyn, a young girl whose brother was killed by an evil dragon, and Simle, a young bronze dragon who hates humans. Sparks will fly when they are thrown together by circumstance in

BRONZE
DRAGON CODEX

Coming July 2008